Old Friends and New

Old Friends and New

Sarah Orne Jewett

MINT EDITIONS

Old Friends and New was first published in 1879.

This edition published by Mint Editions 2021.

ISBN 9781513279855 | E-ISBN 9781513284873

Published by Mint Editions®

MINT
EDITIONS

minteditionbooks.com

Publishing Director: Jennifer Newens
Design & Production: Rachel Lopez Metzger
Project Manager: Micaela Clark
Typesetting: Westchester Publishing Services

Contents

A Lost Lover

For a great many years it had been understood in Longfield that Miss Horatia Dane once had a lover, and that he had been lost at sea. By little and little, in one way and another, her acquaintances had found out or made up the whole story; and Miss Dane stood in the position, not of an unmarried woman exactly, but rather of having spent most of her life in a long and lonely widowhood. She looked like a person with a history, strangers often said (as if we each did not have a history); and her own unbroken reserve about this romance of hers gave everybody the more respect for it.

The Longfield people paid willing deference to Miss Dane: her family had always been one that could be liked and respected, and she was the last that was left in the old home of which she was so fond. This was a high, square house, with a row of pointed windows in its roof, a peaked porch in front, with some lilac-bushes around it; and down by the road was a long, orderly procession of poplars, like a row of sentinels standing guard. She had lived here alone since her father's death, twenty years before. She was a kind, just woman, whose pleasures were of a stately and sober sort; and she seemed not unhappy in her loneliness, though she sometimes said gravely that she was the last of her family, as if the fact had a great sadness for her.

She had some middle-aged and elderly cousins living at a distance, and they came occasionally to see her; but there had been no young people staying in the house for many years until this summer, when the daughter of her youngest cousin had written to ask if she might come to make a visit. She was a motherless girl of twenty, both older and younger than her years. Her father and brother, who were civil engineers, had taken some work upon the line of a railway in the far Western country. Nelly had made many long journeys with them before and since she had left school, and she had meant to follow them now, after she had spent a fortnight with the old cousin whom she had not seen since her childhood. Her father had laughed at the visit as a freak, and had warned her of the dulness and primness of Longfield; but the result was that the girl found herself very happy in the comfortable home. She was still her own free, unfettered, lucky, and sunshiny self; and the old house was so much pleasanter for the girlish face and life, that Miss Horatia had, at first timidly and then most heartily, begged her to stay for the whole summer, or even the autumn, until her father was ready to come East. The name of Dane was very dear to Miss Horatia, and she grew fonder of her guest. When the village-people saw her glance at the girl affectionately, as they sat together in the family-pew of a Sunday, or saw them walking together after tea, they said it was a good thing for Miss Horatia; how bright she looked; and no doubt she would leave all her money to Nelly Dane, if she played her cards well.

But we will do Nelly justice, and say that she was not mercenary: she would have scorned such a thought. She had grown to have a great love for her cousin Horatia, and she liked to please her. She idealized her, I have no doubt; and her repression, her grave courtesy and rare words of approval, had a great fascination for a girl who had just been used to people who chattered, and were upon most intimate terms with you directly, and could forget you with equal ease. And Nelly liked having so admiring and easily pleased an audience as Miss Dane and her old servant Melissa. She liked to be queen of her company: she had so many gay, bright stories of what had happened to herself and her friends. Besides, she was clever with her needle, and had all those practical gifts which elderly women approve so heartily in girls. They liked her pretty clothes; she was sensible and economical and busy; they praised her to each other and to the world, and even stubborn old Andrew, the man, to whom Miss Horatia herself spoke with deference, would do any thing she asked. Nelly would by no means choose so dull a life as this for the rest of her days; but she enjoyed it immensely for the time being. She instinctively avoided all that would shock the grave dignity and old-school ideas of Miss Dane; and somehow she never had felt happier or better satisfied with life. I think it was because she was her best and most lady-like self. It was not long before she knew the village-people almost as well as Miss Dane did, and she became a very great favorite, as a girl so easily can who is good-natured and pretty, and well versed in city fashions; who has that tact and cleverness that come to such a nature from going about the world and knowing many people.

She had not been in Longfield many weeks before she heard something of Miss Dane's love-story; for one of her new friends said, in a confidential moment, "Does your cousin ever speak to you about the young man to whom she was engaged to be married?" And Nelly answered, "No," with great wonder, and not without regret at her own ignorance. After this she kept her eyes and ears open for whatever news of this lover's existence might be found.

At last it happened one day that she had a good chance for a friendly talk with Melissa; for who should know about the family affairs better than she? Miss Horatia had taken her second-best parasol, with a deep fringe, and had gone majestically down the street to do some morning errands which she could trust to no one. Melissa was shelling peas at the shady kitchen-doorstep, and Nelly came strolling round from the garden, along the clean-swept flag-stones, and sat down to help her. Melissa moved along, with a grim smile, to make room for her. "You needn't bother yourself," said she: "I've nothing else to do. You'll green your fingers all over." But she was evidently pleased to have company.

"My fingers will wash," said Nelly, "and I've nothing else to do either. Please push the basket this way a little, or I shall scatter the pods, and then you will scold." She went to work busily, while she tried to think of the best way to find out the story she wished to hear.

"There!" said Melissa, "I never told Miss H'ratia to get some citron, and I settled yesterday to make some pound-cake this forenoon after I got dinner along a piece. She's most out o' mustard too; she's set about having mustard to eat with her beef, just as the old colonel was before her. I never saw any other folks eat mustard with their roast beef; but every family has their own tricks. I tied a thread round my left-hand little finger purpose to remember that citron before she came down this morning. I hope I ain't losing my fac'lties." It was seldom that Melissa was so talkative as this at first. She was clearly in a talkative mood.

"Melissa," asked Nelly, with great bravery, after a minute or two of silence, "who was it that my cousin Horatia was going to many? It's odd that I shouldn't know; but I don't remember father's ever speaking of it, and I shouldn't think of asking her."

"I s'pose it'll seem strange to you," said Melissa, beginning to shell the peas a great deal faster, "but, as many years as I have lived in this house with her,—her mother, the old lady, fetched me up,—I never knew Miss H'ratia to say a word about him. But there! she knows I know, and we've got an understanding on many things we never talk over as some folks would. I've heard about it from other folks. She was visiting her great-aunt in Salem when she met with him. His name was Carrick, and it was presumed they was going to be married when he came home from the voyage he was lost on. He had the promise of going out master of a new ship. They didn't keep company long: it was made up of a sudden, and folks here didn't get hold of the story till some time after. I've heard some that ought to know say it was only talk, and they never were engaged to be married no more than I am."

"You say he was lost at sea?" asked Nelly.

"The ship never was heard from. They supposed she was run down in the night out in the South Seas somewhere. It was a good while before they gave up expecting news; but none ever come. I think she set every thing by him, and took it very hard losing of him. But there! she'd never say a word. You're the freest-spoken Dane I ever saw; but you may take it from 'our mother's folks. I know he gave her that whale's tooth with the ship drawn on it that's on the mantel-piece in her room. She may have a sight of other keepsakes, for all I know; but it ain't likely." And here there was a pause, in which Nelly grew sorrowful as she thought of the long waiting for tidings of the missing ship, and of her cousin's solitary life. It was very odd to think of prim Miss Horatia's being in love with a sailor. There was a young lieutenant in the navy whom Nelly herself liked dearly, and he had gone away on a long voyage. "Perhaps she's been just as well off," said Melissa. "She's dreadful set, y'r cousin H'ratia is, and sailors is high-tempered men. I've heard it hinted that he was a fast fellow; and if a woman's got a good home like this, and's able to do for herself, she'd better stay there. I ain't going to give up a certainty for an uncertainty,—that's what *I* always tell 'em," added Melissa, with great decision, as if she were besieged by lovers; but Nelly smiled inwardly as she thought of the courage it would take to support any one who wished to offer her companion his heart and hand. It would need desperate energy to scale the walls of that garrison.

The green peas were all shelled presently, and Melissa said gravely that she should have to be lazy now until it was time to put in the meat. She wasn't used to being helped, unless there was extra work, and she calculated to have one piece of work join on to another. However, it was no account, and she was obliged for the company; and Nelly laughed merrily as she stood washing her hands in the shining old copper basin at the sink. The sun would not be round that side of the house for a long time yet, and the pink and blue morning-glories were still in their full bloom and freshness. They grew over the window, twined on strings exactly the same distance apart. There was a box crowded full of green houseleeks down at the side of the door: they were straying over the edge, and Melissa stooped stiffly down with an air of disapproval at their untidiness. "They straggle all over every thing," said she, "and they're no kind of use, only Miss's mother she set every thing by 'em. She fetched 'em from home with her when she was married, her mother kep' a box, and they came from England. Folks used to say they was good for bee-stings." Then she went into the inner kitchen, and Nelly went slowly away along the flag-stones to the garden from whence she had come. The garden-gate opened with a tired creak, and shut with a clack; and she noticed how smooth and shiny the wood was where the touch of so many hands had worn it. There was a great pleasure to this girl in finding herself among such old and well-worn things. She had been for a long time in cities or at the West; and among the old fashions and ancient possessions of Long-field it seemed to her that every thing had its story, and she liked the quietness and unchangeableness with which life seemed to go on from year to year. She had seen many a dainty or gorgeous garden, but never one that she had liked so well as this, with its herb-bed and its broken rows of currant-bushes, its tall stalks of white lilies and its wandering rose-bushes and honeysuckles, that had bloomed beside the straight paths for so many more summers than she herself had lived. She picked a little nosegay of late red roses, and carried it into the house to put on the parlor-table. The wide hall-door was standing open, with its green outer blinds closed, and the old hall was dim and cool. Miss Horatia did not like a glare of sunlight, and she abhorred flies with her whole heart. Nelly could hardly see her way through the rooms, it had been so bright out of doors; but she brought the tall champagne-glass of water from the dining-room and put the flowers in their place. Then she looked at two silhouettes which stood on the mantel in carved ebony frames. They were portraits of an uncle of Miss Dane and his wife. Miss Dane had thought Nelly looked like this uncle the evening before. She could not see the likeness herself; but the pictures suggested something else, and she turned suddenly, and went hurrying up the stairs to Miss Horatia's own room, where she remembered to have seen a group of silhouettes fastened to the wall. There were seven or eight, and she looked at the young men among them most carefully; but they were all marked with the name of Dane: they were Miss Horatia's brothers, and our friend hung them on their little brass hooks again with a feeling of disappointment. Perhaps her cousin had a quaint miniature of the lover, painted on ivory, and shut in a worn red morocco case; she hoped she should get a sight of it some day. This story of the lost sailor had a wonderful charm for the girl. Miss Horatia had never been so interesting to her before. How she must have mourned for the lover, and missed him, and hoped there would yet be news from the ship! Nelly thought she would tell her her own little love-story some day, though there was not much to tell yet, in spite of there being so much to think about. She built a little castle in Spain as she sat in the front-window-seat of the upper hall, and dreamed pleasant stories for herself until the sharp noise of the front-gate-latch waked her; and she looked out through the blind to see her cousin coming up the walk.

Miss Horatia looked hot and tired, and her thoughts were not of any fashion of romance. "It is going to be very warm," said she. "I have been worrying ever since I have been gone, because I forgot to ask Andrew to pick those white currants for the minister's wife. I promised that she should have them early this morning. Would you go out to the kitchen, and ask Melissa to step in for a moment, my dear?"

Melissa was picking over red currants to make a pie, and rose from her chair with a little unwillingness. "I guess they could wait until afternoon," said she, as she came back. "Miss H'ratia's in a fret because she forgot about sending some white currants to the minister's. I told her that Andrew had gone to have the horses shod, and wouldn't be back till near noon. I don't see why part of the folks in the world should kill themselves trying to suit the rest. As long as I haven't got any citron for the cake, I suppose I might go out and pick 'em," added Melissa ungraciously. "I'll get some to set away for tea anyhow."

Miss Dane had a letter to write after she had rested from her walk; and Nelly soon left her in the dark parlor, and went back to the sunshiny garden to help Melissa, who seemed to be taking life with more than her usual disapproval. She was sheltered by an enormous gingham sunbonnet.

"I set out to free my mind to your cousin H'ratia this morning," said she, as Nelly crouched down at the opposite side of the bush where she was picking; "but we can't agree on that p'int, and it's no use. I don't say nothing. You might's well ask the moon to face about and travel the other way as to try to change Miss H'ratia's mind. I ain't going to argue it with her: it ain't my place; I know that as well as anybody. She'd run her feet off for the minister's folks any day; and, though I do say he's a fair preacher, they haven't got a speck o' consideration nor fac'lty; they think the world was made for them, but I think likely they'll find out it wasn't; most folks do. When he first was settled here, I had a fit o' sickness, and he come to see me when I was getting over the worst of it. He did the best he could, I always took it very kind of him; but he made a prayer, and he kep' sayin' 'this aged handmaid,' I should think, a dozen times. Aged handmaid!" said Melissa scornfully: "I don't call myself aged yet, and that was more than ten years ago. I never made pretensions to being younger than I am; but you'd 'a' thought I was a topplin' old creatur' going on a hundred."

Nelly laughed; Melissa looked cross, and moved on to the next currant-bush. "So that's why you don't like the minister?" But the question did not seem to please.

"I hope I never should be set against a preacher by such as that." And Nelly hastened to change the subject; but there was to be a last word: "I like to see a minister that's solid minister right straight through, not one of these veneered folks. But old Parson Croden spoilt me for setting under any other preaching."

"I wonder," said Nelly, after a little, "if Cousin Horatia has any picture of that Captain Carrick."

"He wasn't captain," said Melissa. "I never heard that it was any more than they talked of giving him a ship next voyage."

"And you never saw him? He never came here to see her?"

"Bless you, no! She met with him at Salem, where she was spending the winter, and he went right away to sea. I've heard a good deal more about it of late years than I ever did at the time. I suppose the Salem folks talked about it enough. All I know is, there was other good matches that offered to her since, and couldn't get her; and I suppose it was on account of her heart's being buried in the deep with him." And this unexpected bit of sentiment, spoken in Melissa's grummest tone, seemed so funny to her young companion, that she bent very low to pick from a currant-twig close to the ground, and could not ask any more questions for some time.

"I have seen her a sight o' times when I knew she was thinking about him," Melissa went on presently, this time with a tenderness in her voice that touched Nelly's heart. "She's been dreadful lonesome. She and the old colonel, her father, wasn't much company to each other, and she always kep' every thing to herself. The only time she ever said a word to me was one night six or seven years ago this Christmas. They got up a Christmas-tree in the vestry, and she went, and I did too; I guess everybody in the whole church and parish that could crawl turned out to go. The children they made a dreadful racket. I'd ha' got my ears took off if I had been so forth-putting when

I was little. I was looking round for Miss H'ratia 'long at the last of the evening, and somebody said they'd seen her go home. I hurried, and I couldn't see any light in the house; and I was afraid she was sick or something. She come and let me in, and I see she had been a-cryin'. I says, 'Have you heard any bad news?' But she says, 'No,' and began to cry again, real pitiful. 'I never felt so lonesome in my life,' says she, 'as I did down there. It's a dreadful thing to be left all alone in the world.' I did feel for her; but I couldn't seem to say a word. I put some pine-chips I had handy for morning on the kitchen-fire, and I made her up a cup o' good hot tea quick's I could, and took it to her; and I guess she felt better. She never went to bed till three o'clock that night. I couldn't shut my eyes till I heard her come upstairs. There! I set every thing by Miss H'ratia. I haven't got no folks either. I was left an orphan over to Deerfield, where Miss's mother come from, and she took me out o' the town-farm to bring up. I remember, when I come here, I was so small I had a box to stand up on when I helped wash the dishes. There's nothing I ain't had to make me comfortable, and I do just as I'm a mind to, and call in extra help every day of the week if I give the word; but I've had my lonesome times, and I guess Miss H'ratia knew."

Nelly was very much touched by this bit of a story, it was a new idea to her that Melissa should have so much affection and be so sympathetic. People never will get over being surprised that chestnut-burrs are not as rough inside as they are outside, and the girl's heart warmed toward the old woman who had spoken with such unlooked-for sentiment and pathos. Melissa went to the house with her basket, and Nelly also went in, but only to put on another hat, and see if it were straight, in a minute spent before the old mirror, and then she hurried down the long elm-shaded street to buy a pound of citron for the cake. She left it on the kitchen-table when she came back, and nobody ever said any thing about it; only there were two delicious pound-cakes—a heart and a round—on a little blue china plate beside Nelly's plate at tea.

After tea Nelly and Miss Dane sat in the front-doorway,—the elder woman in a high-backed arm-chair, and the younger on the doorstep. The tree-toads and crickets were tuning up heartily, the stars showed a little through the trees, and the elms looked heavy and black against the sky. The fragrance of the white lilies in the garden blew through the hall. Miss Horatia was tapping the ends of her fingers together. Probably she was not thinking of any thing in particular. She had had a very peaceful day, with the exception of the currants; and they had, after all, gone to the parsonage some time before noon. Beside this, the minister had sent word that the delay made no trouble; for his wife had unexpectedly gone to Downton to pass the day and night. Miss Horatia had received the business-letter for which she had been looking for several days; so there was nothing to regret deeply for that day, and there seemed to be nothing for one to dread on the morrow.

"Cousin Horatia," asked Nelly, "are you sure you like having me here? Are you sure I don't trouble you?"

"Of course not," said Miss Dane, without a bit of sentiment in her tone: "I find it very pleasant having young company, though I am used to being alone; and I don't mind it so much as I suppose you would."

"I should mind it very much," said the girl softly.

"You would get used to it, as I have," said Miss Dane. "Yes, dear, I like having you here better and better. I hate to think of your going away." And she smoothed Nelly's hair as if she thought she might have spoken coldly at first, and wished to make up for it. This rare caress was not without its effect.

"I don't miss father and Dick so very much," owned Nelly frankly, "because I have grown used to their coming and going; but sometimes I miss people—Cousin Horatia, did I ever say any thing to you about George Forest?"

"I think I remember the name," answered Miss Dane.

"He is in the navy, and he has gone a long voyage, and—I think every thing of him. I missed him awfully; but it is almost time to get a letter from him."

"Does your father approve of him?" asked Miss Dane, with great propriety. "You are very young yet, and you must not think of such a thing carelessly. I should be so much grieved if you threw away your happiness."

"Oh! we are not really engaged," said Nelly, who felt a little chilled. "I suppose we are, too: only nobody knows yet. Yes, father knows him as well as I do, and he is very fond of him. Of course I should not keep it from father; but he guessed at it himself. Only it's such a long cruise, Cousin Horatia,—three years, I suppose,—away off in China and Japan."

"I have known longer voyages than that," said Miss Dane, with a quiver in her voice; and she rose suddenly, and walked away, this grave, reserved woman, who seemed so contented and so comfortable. But, when she came back, she asked Nelly a great deal about her lover, and learned more of the girl's life than she ever had before. And they talked together in the pleasantest way about this pleasant subject, which was so close to Nelly's heart, until Melissa brought the candles at ten o'clock, that being the hour of Miss Dane's bed-time.

But that night Miss Dane did not go to bed at ten: she sat by the window in her room, thinking. The moon rose late; and after a little while she blew out her candles, which were burning low. I suppose that the years which had come and gone since the young sailor went away on that last voyage of his had each added to her affection for him. She was a person who clung the more fondly to youth as she left it the farther behind.

This is such a natural thing: the great sorrows of our youth sometimes become the amusements of our later years; we can only remember them with a smile. We find that our lives look fairer to us, and we forget what used to trouble us so much when we look back. Miss Dane certainly had come nearer to truly loving the sailor than she had any one else; and the more she had thought of it, the more it became the romance of her life. She no longer asked herself, as she often had done in middle life, whether, if he had lived and had come home, she would have loved and married him. She had minded less and less, year by year, knowing that her friends and neighbors thought her faithful to the love of her youth. Poor, gay, handsome Joe Carrick! how fond he had been of her, and how he had looked at her that day he sailed away out of Salem Harbor on the ship Chevalier! If she had only known that she never should see him again, poor fellow!

But, as usual, her thoughts changed their current a little at the end of her reverie. Perhaps, after all, loneliness was not so hard to bear as other sorrows. She had had a pleasant life, God had been very good to her, and had spared her many trials, and granted her many blessings. She would try and serve him better. "I am an old woman now," she said to herself. "Things are better as they are; God knows best, and I never should have liked to be interfered with."

Then she shut out the moonlight, and lighted her candles again, with an almost guilty feeling. "What should I say if Nelly sat up till nearly midnight looking out at the moon?" thought she. "It is very silly; but it is such a beautiful night. I should like to have her see the moon shining through the tops of the trees." But Nelly was sleeping the sleep of the just and sensible in her own room.

Next morning at breakfast Nelly was a little conscious of there having been uncommon confidences the night before; but Miss Dane was her usual calm and somewhat formal self, and proposed their making a few calls after dinner, if the weather were not too hot. Nelly at once wondered what she had better wear. There was a certain black grenadine which Miss Horatia had noticed with approval, and she remembered that the lower ruffle needed hemming, and made up her mind that she would devote most of the time before dinner to that and to some other repairs. So, after breakfast was over, she brought the dress downstairs, with her work-box, and settled herself in the dining-room. Miss Dane usually sat there in the morning, it was a pleasant room, and she could keep an unsuspected watch over the kitchen and Melissa, who did not need watching in the least. I dare say it was for the sake of being within the sound of a voice.

Miss Dane marched in and out that morning; she went upstairs, and came down again, and she was busy for a while in the parlor. Nelly was sewing steadily by a window, where one of the blinds was a little way open, and tethered in its place by a string. She hummed a tune to herself over and over:—

> *"What will you do, love, when I am going,*
> *With white sails flowing, the seas beyond?"*

And old Melissa, going to and fro at her work in the kitchen, grumbled out bits of an ancient psalm-tune at intervals. There seemed to be some connection between these fragments in her mind; it was like a ledge of rock in a pasture, that sometimes runs under the ground, and then crops out again. I think it was the tune of Windham.

Nelly found there was a good deal to be done to the grenadine dress when she looked it over critically, and she was very diligent. It was quiet in and about the house for a long time, until suddenly she heard the sound of heavy footsteps coming in from the road. The side-door was in a little entry between the room where Nelly sat and the kitchen, and the new-comer knocked loudly. "A tramp," said Nelly to herself; while Melissa came to open the door, wiping her hands hurriedly on her apron.

"I wonder if you couldn't give me something to eat," said the man.

"I suppose I could," answered Melissa. "Will you step in?" Beggars were very few in Longfield, and Miss Dane never wished anybody to go away hungry from her house. It was off the grand highway of tramps; but they were by no means unknown.

Melissa searched among her stores, and Nelly heard her putting one plate after another on the kitchen-table, and thought that the breakfast promised to be a good one, if it were late.

"Don't put yourself out," said the man, as he moved his chair nearer. "I put up at an old barn three or four miles above here last night, and there didn't seem to be very good board there."

"Going far?" inquired Melissa concisely.

"Boston," said the man. "I'm a little too old to travel afoot. Now, if I could go by water, it would seem nearer. I'm more used to the water. This is a royal good piece o' beef. I suppose couldn't put your hand on a mug of cider?" This was said humbly; but the tone failed to touch Melissa's heart.

"No, I couldn't," said she decisively; so there was an end of that, and the conversation seemed to flag for a time.

Presently Melissa came to speak to Miss Dane, who had just come downstairs. "Could you stay in the kitchen a few minutes?" she whispered. "There's an old creatur' there that looks foreign. He came to the door for something to eat, and I gave it to him; but he's miser'ble looking, and I don't like to leave him alone. I'm just in the midst o' dressing the chickens. He'll be through pretty quick, according to the way he's eating now."

Miss Dane followed her without a word; and the man half rose, and said, "Good-morning, madam!" with unusual courtesy. And, when Melissa was out of hearing, he spoke again: "I suppose you haven't any cider?" to which his hostess answered, "I couldn't give you any this morning," in a tone that left no room for argument. He looked as if he had had a great deal too much to drink already.

"How far do you call it from here to Boston?" he asked, and was told that it was eighty miles.

"I'm a slow traveller," said he: "sailors don't take much to walking." Miss Dane asked him if he had been a sailor. "Nothing else," replied the man, who seemed much inclined to talk. He had been eating like a hungry dog, as if he were half-starved,—a slouching, red-faced, untidy-looking old man, with some traces of former good looks still to be discovered in his face. "Nothing else. I ran away to sea when I was a boy, and I followed it until I got so old they wouldn't ship me even for cook." There was something in his being for once so comfortable—perhaps it was being with a lady like Miss Dane, who pitied him—that lifted his thoughts a little from their usual low level. "It's drink that's been the ruin of me," said he. "I ought to have been somebody. I was nobody's fool when I was young. I got to be mate of a first-rate ship, and there was some talk o' my being captain before long. She was lost that voyage, and three of us were all that was saved; we got picked up by a Chinese junk. She had the plague aboard of her, and my mates died of it, and I was sick. It was a hell of a place to be in. When I got ashore I shipped on an old bark that pretended to be coming round the Cape, and she turned out to be a pirate. I just went to the dogs, and I've been from bad to worse ever since."

"It's never too late to mend," said Melissa, who came into the kitchen just then for a string to tie the chickens.

"Lord help us, yes, it is!" said the sailor. "It's easy for you to say that. I'm too old. I ain't been master of this craft for a good while." And he laughed at his melancholy joke.

"Don't say that," said Miss Dane.

"Well, now, what could an old wrack like me do to earn a living? and who'd want me if I could? You wouldn't. I don't know when I've been treated so decent as this before. I'm all broke down." But his tone was no longer sincere; he had fallen back on his profession of beggar.

"Couldn't you get into some asylum or—there's the Sailors' Snug Harbor, isn't that for men like you? It seems such a pity for a man of your years to be homeless and a wanderer. Haven't you any friends at all?" And here, suddenly, Miss Dane's face altered, and she grew very white; something startled her. She looked as one might who saw a fearful ghost.

"No," said the man; "but my folks used to be some of the best in Salem. I haven't shown my head there this good while. I was an orphan. My grandmother brought me up. Why, I didn't come back to the States for thirty or forty years. Along at the first of it I used to see men in port that I used to know; but I always dodged 'em, and I was way off in outlandish places. I've got an awful sight to answer for. I used to have a good wife when I was in Australia. I don't know where I haven't been, first and last. I was always a hard fellow. I've spent as much as a couple o' fortunes, and here I am. Devil take it!"

Nelly was still sewing in the dining-room; but, soon after Miss Dane had gone out to the kitchen, one of the doors between had slowly closed itself with a plaintive whine. The round stone that Melissa used to keep it open had been pushed away. Nelly was a little annoyed: she liked to hear what was going on; but she was just then holding her work with great care in a place that was hard to sew; so she did not move. She heard the murmur of voices, and thought, after a while, that the old vagabond ought to go away by this time. What could be making her cousin Horatia talk so long with him? It was not like her at all. He would beg for money, of course, and she hoped Miss Horatia would not give him a single cent.

It was some time before the kitchen-door opened, and the man came out with clumsy, stumbling steps. "I'm much obliged to you," he said, "and I don't know but it is the last time I'll get treated as if I was a gentleman. Is there any thing I could do for you round the place?" he asked hesitatingly, and as if he hoped that his offer would not be accepted.

"No," answered Miss Dane. "No, thank you. Good-by!" and he went away.

I said he had been lifted a little above his low life; he fell back again directly before he was out of the gate. "I'm blessed if she didn't give me a ten-dollar bill!" said he. "She must have thought it was one. I'll get out o' call as quick as I can, hope she won't find it out, and send anybody after me." Visions of unlimited drinks, and other things in which the old sailor found pleasure, flitted through his stupid mind. "How the old lady stared at me once!" he thought. "Wonder if she was anybody I used to know? 'Downton?' I don't know as I ever heard of the place." And he scuffed along the dusty road; and that night he was very drunk, and the next day he went wandering on, God only knows where.

But Nelly and Melissa both had heard a strange noise in the kitchen, as if some one had fallen, and had found that Miss Horatia had fainted dead away. It was partly the heat, she said, when she saw their anxious faces as she came to herself; she had had a little headache all the morning; it was very hot and close in the kitchen, and the faintness had come upon her suddenly. They helped her walk into the cool parlor presently, and Melissa brought her a glass of wine, and Nelly sat beside her on a footstool as she lay on the sofa, and fanned her. Once she held her cheek against Miss Horatia's hand for a minute, and she will never know as long as she lives what a comfort she was that day.

Every one but Miss Dane forgot the old sailor-tramp in this excitement that followed his visit. Do you guess already who he was? But the certainty could not come to you with the chill and horror it did to Miss Dane. There had been something familiar in his look and voice from the first, and then she had suddenly known him, her lost lover.

It was an awful change that the years had made in him. He had truly called himself a wreck: he was like some dreary wreck in its decay and utter ruin, its miserable ugliness and worthlessness, falling to pieces in the slow tides of a lifeless southern sea.

And he had once been her lover, Miss Dane thought many times in the days that came after. Not that there was ever any thing asked or promised between them, but they had liked each other dearly, and had parted with deep sorrow. She had thought of him all these years so tenderly; she had believed always that his love had been greater than her own, and never once had doubted that the missing ship Chevalier had carried with it down into the sea a heart that was true to her.

By little and little this all grew familiar, and she accustomed herself to the knowledge of her new secret. She shuddered at the thought of the misery of a life with him, and she thanked God for sparing her such shame and despair. The distance between them seemed immense. She had been a person of so much consequence among her friends, and so dutiful and irreproachable a woman. She had not begun to understand what dishonor is in the world; her life had been shut in by safe and orderly surroundings. It was a strange chance that had brought this wanderer to her door. She remembered his wretched untidiness. She would not have liked even to touch him. She had never imagined him grown old: he had always been young to her. It was a great mercy he had not known her; it would have been a most miserable position for them both; and yet she thought, with sad surprise, that she had not known she had changed so entirely. She thought of the different ways their roads in life had gone; she pitied him; she cried about him more than once; and she wished that she could know he was dead. He might have been such a brave, good man, with his strong will and resolute courage. God forgive him for the wickedness which his strength had been made to serve! "God forgive him!" said Miss Horatia to herself sadly over and over again. She wondered if she ought to have let him go away, and so have lost sight of him; but she could not do any thing else. She suffered terribly on his account; she had a pity, such as God's pity must be, for even his wilful sins.

So her romance was all over with; yet the towns-people still whispered it to strangers, and even Melissa and Nelly never knew how she had lost her lover in so strange and sad a way in her latest years. Nobody noticed much change; but Melissa saw that the whale's tooth had disappeared from its place in Miss Horatia's room, and her old friends said to each other that she began to show her age a great deal. She seemed really like an old woman now; she was not the woman she had been a year ago.

This is all of the story; but I so often wish when a story comes to an end that I knew what became of the people afterward. Shall I tell you that Miss Horatia clings more and more fondly to her young cousin Nelly; and that Nelly will stay with her a great deal before she marries, and sometimes afterward, when the lieutenant goes away to sea? Shall I say that Miss Dane seems as well satisfied and comfortable as ever, though she acknowledges she is not so young as she used to be, and somehow misses something out of her life? It is the contentment of winter rather than that of summer: the flowers are out of bloom for her now, and under the snow. And Melissa, will not she always be the same, with a quaintness and freshness and toughness like a cedar-tree, to the end of her days? Let us hope they will live on together and be untroubled this long time yet, the two good women; and let us wish Nelly much pleasure, and a sweet soberness and fearlessness as she grows older and finds life a harder thing to understand and a graver thing to know.

A Sorrowful Guest

Dear Helen,

What do you say to our going to housekeeping together? I'm a very old bachelor, with many whims; but I'm your brother, and I don't know that there was ever an act of Parliament that we should spend our lives on opposite shores of the Atlantic. The Athertons' lease of our house is out next month, and I have a fancy for taking it myself. We will call it merely an experiment, if you like; but I'm tired of the way I live now. I'm growing gray, and I shall be dreadfully glad to see you. We will make a real home of it, and see something of each other; you must not ask for any more pathos than this. Pick up whatever you can to make the house look fine, but don't feel in the least obliged to come, or put it off until the spring. Do just as you like. I hear the Duncans are coming home in October; perhaps you could take passage on the same steamer. I can't believe it is three years since I went over last. Do you think we shall know each other? *"L'absence diminue les petits amours et augmente les grandes, comme le vent qui éteint les bougies et rallume la feu."* I met that sentiment in a story I was reading to-day, and I thought it would seem very gallant and alluring if I put it into my letter. I think you will not be homesick here: you will find more friends than seems possible at first thought. I'm in a hurry to-day; but I'm none the less

Your very affectionate brother,
JOHN AINSLIE
Boston, Aug. 2, 1877

This was a letter which came to me one morning a year or two ago from my only brother. We had been separated most of the time since our childhood; for my father and mother both died then, and our home was broken up, as Jack was to be away at school and college. During the war he was fired with a love of his country and a longing for military glory, and entered the army with many of his fellow-students at Harvard. I was at school for a time, but afterwards went to live with an aunt, whose winter home was in Florence; and when Jack left the army he came to Europe to go on with his professional studies. He was most of the time in Dublin and London and Paris at the medical schools; but we were together a good deal, and he went off for several long journeys with my aunt and me before he went back to America. I always hoped that we might some day live together: but my aunt wished me never to leave her; for she was somewhat of an invalid, and had grown to depend on me more or less in many ways. She could not live in Boston, for the climate did not suit her. If Jack and I had not written each other so often, we should have drifted far apart; but, as it was, I think our love and friendship grew closer year by year. I should have begged him to come to live with me; but he was always in a hurry to get back to his own city and his own friends when he sometimes came over to pay us a visit in my aunt's lifetime, and I knew he would not be contented in Florence.

At Aunt Alice's death I went on with the same old life for a time from force of habit; and it was just then, when I was with some friends in the Tyrol, and had been wondering what plans I should make for the winter,—whether to go to Egypt again, or to have some English friends come to me in Florence,—that Jack's letter came. I was only too glad that he made the proposal, and I could not resist sending him a cable despatch to say, "Hurrah!" I had not realized before how lonely and adrift I had felt since Aunt Alice died. I had a host of kind friends; but there is nothing like being with one's own kindred, and having one's own home. It was very hard work to say so many good-byes; and my heart had almost failed me when I saw some of my friends for, it might be, the last time, as some of them were old people. And, though I said over and over again that I should come back in a year or two, who could be certain that I should take up the dear familiar life again? But, though I had been so many long years away from dear old Boston, I never had been so glad in my life to catch sight of any city as I was that chilly, late October morning, when I came on deck, and somebody pointed out to me a dull glitter of something that looked higher and brighter than the land, and said it was the dome of the State House.

I felt more sure than ever that I was going home when I saw my brother standing on the wharf, and I remembered so clearly many of the streets we drove through; and when we came to the house itself, and the carriage had gone, and we stood in the library together where the very same books were in the cases, and the same dim old Turkey carpet on the floor, the years seemed suddenly to vanish, and it was like the dear old childish days again: only where were my mother and my father? And Jack was growing gray, as he had written me, and so much had happened to me since I had been in that room last! I sat down before the wood-fire; and the queer brass dragons on the andirons made me smile, just as they always used. Jack stood at the window, looking out; and neither of us had a word to say, though we had chattered at each other every minute as we drove over from the steamer.

That first evening at dinner I looked across the table at my brother: and our eyes met, and we both laughed heartily for very contentment and delight.

"I'm sure Aunt Marion ought to be here to matronize you," said Jack. Neither of us like Aunt Marion very well; and this was a great joke, especially as she was ushered in directly to welcome me home.

Jack had been living at the house for a few weeks already; but it was great fun, this beginning our housekeeping together, and we were busy enough for some time. I had brought over a good many things that my aunt had had in Florence, and to which I had become attached; and in the course of many journeys both Jack and I had accumulated a great many large and small treasures, some of which had not been unpacked for years. I very soon knew my brother's best friends; and we both tried to make our home not only cheerful and bright and pleasant in every way, but we wished also to make it a home-like place, where people might be sure of finding at least some sympathy and true friendliness and help as well as pleasure. Mamma's old friends were charmingly kind and polite to me; and, as Jack had foretold, I found more acquaintances of my own than I had the least idea I should. I had met abroad a great many of the people who came to see me; but the strangest thing was to meet those whom I remembered as my playmates and schoolmates, and to find them so entirely grown up, most of them married, and with homes and children of their own instead of the playhouses and dolls which I remembered.

We soon fell into a most comfortable fashion of living, we were both very fond of giving quiet little dinners, my brother often brought home a friend or two, and we were charmingly independent; life never went better with two people than it did with Jack and me. We often had some old friends of the family come to stay with us, and I sent hither and yon for my own old cronies, with some of whom I had kept up our friendship since school-days; and, while it was not a little sad to meet some of them again, with others I felt as if we had only parted yesterday.

I had been curious to know many things about Jack, and I found I had been right in supposing that his profession was by no means a burden to him. I was told again and again that he was a wonderfully successful and daring surgeon; but he confessed to me that his dislike to such work continually increased, and could only be overcome in the excitement of some desperate emergency. It seemed to me at first that he ought not to let his skill lie useless and idle; but he insisted that the other doctors did as well as he, that they sent for him if they wanted him, and he did not care for a practice of his own. So he had grown into a way of helping his friends with their business; and he was a microscopist of some renown, and a scientific man, instead of the practical man he ought to have been,—though his was, after all, by no means an idle nor a useless life, dear old Jack! He did a great deal of good shyly and quietly; he was often at the hospitals, and his friends seemed very fond of him, and said he had too little confidence in himself. I have often wondered why he did not marry; but I doubt if he ever tells me, though he knows well enough my own story, and that there is a quiet grave in Florence which is always in sight, no matter how far away from it I go, while sometimes I think I know every ivy-leaf that falls on it from the wall near by.

As I have said, my brother was constantly meeting some one of his old classmates or army comrades or school friends during that first winter; and, while sometimes he would ask them to dine at his club, he oftener brought them home to dine or to lunch; for we were both possessed with an amazing spirit of hospitality. I wish I could remember half the stories I have heard, or could keep track of the lives in which I often grew much interested. There is one curious story which I knew, and which seems very well worth telling,—an instance of the curious entanglement of two lives, and of those strange experiences which some people call supernatural, and others think simple enough and perfectly reasonable and explainable.

One short, snowy December day, just as it was growing dark, I was sitting alone in the library, and was surprised to hear my brother's latch-key click in the hall-door; for he had told me, when he went out after our very late breakfast, that he should not be in before six, and perhaps dinner had better wait until seven. He threw off his wet ulster, and was talking for some time to the man, and at last came in to me.

"What brings you home so early?" said I.

"I'm going to have two or three friends to dine. I suppose it'll be all right about the dinner? That was not why I came home, though: I had some letters to write which must go by the steamer, and I didn't go to Cambridge after all. The snow-storm was too much for me, I wanted a good light there."

"Sit down a while," said I. "You have time enough for your letters; it's only a little after four." Jack hated to write at the library-table, and always went to the desk in his own book-room if he had any thing to do. He seemed a little tired, and threw me some letters the postman had given him as he came in at the door; then he sat down in his great chair near me, and seemed to be lost in thought. He was immensely interesting to me then; for we had only been together a few weeks, and I was often curious about his moods, and was apt to be much pained myself if any thing seemed to trouble him. I was always wishing we had not been separated so much, and I was afraid I might be wanting in insight and sympathy; but I think the truth has been that we are much more intimate, and are far better friends, and have less restraint, because we had seen so little of one another in the years that had passed. But we were terribly afraid of interfering with each other at first, and were so distractingly polite that we bored each other not a little; though that did not last long, happily, after we had convinced each other that we could behave well.

"You say it'll be all right about dinner?" repeated my brother.

"Oh, yes!" said I, "unless you wish for something very grand. Would you like to have me put on my crown and sceptre?"

"There has never been a day yet when I should have been sorry to have brought a friend home," said Jack, with a good deal of enthusiasm, and I was at once puffed up with pride; for Jack, though an uncomplaining soul, was also fastidious, and his praise was not given often enough to be unnoticed.

"I met an old classmate just now," said he presently, rousing himself from his reverie. "I haven't seen him for years before. He went out to South America just after the war, and I supposed he was there still. He used to be one of the best fellows in the class; and he enlisted when I did, though we did not belong to the same company. I heard once he was rather a failure; but something has broken him down horribly. He doesn't look as if he drank," said my brother, half to himself. "I met him over on Tremont Street, and I think he meant to avoid me; but I made him walk across the Common with me, for he was coming this way. He promised to come to dinner this evening; and I stopped at the club a few minutes as I came down the street, and luckily found George

Sheffield, and he is coming round too. I told him seven o'clock, but I told Whiston we dined at six, without thinking; so he will be here early. Never mind: I'll be ready, and we will take care of ourselves. I must finish my letters, though," and he rose from his chair to go upstairs. "It is dreadful to see a man change so," said Jack, still lingering. "He used to be one of the friskiest fellows in college. I hope he'll come. I didn't exactly like to ask where I could find him."

Then he went away: and I waited awhile, looking out at the snow, and thinking idly enough, until Patrick came silently in, and surprised me with a sudden blaze of gas; when I went upstairs to dress for dinner, as there didn't seem to be any thing else to do. I was a little sorry that any one was coming. Jack and I had arranged for a quiet evening together, and he was reading some new book aloud in which I was much interested. His reading was a perfect delight to me. He did not force you to think how well he read, but rather how charming the story or the poem was; and I always liked Jack's voice.

I found something to be busy about in my room, and did not come down again until some time after six. When I entered the parlor, Jack arose with a satisfied smile, and presented Mr. Whiston; and I was pleasantly surprised, for I had half expected to see a most forlorn-looking man, perhaps even out at elbows, from what Jack had said. He was very pale indeed, and looked like an invalid; and he certainly looked frightened and miserable. He had a hunted look. It was the face I should imagine one would have who was haunted by the memory of some awful crime; but I both pitied him and liked him very much.

He said he remembered seeing me one day out at Cambridge with my brother when I was hardly more than a child; and we talked about those old days until my cousin George Sheffield came, Jack's best friend, who had also been Mr. Whiston's classmate.

I fancied, as we went out to dinner, that our guest would enjoy the evening, his friends were giving him so hearty and cordial a welcome; and I was glad the table looked so bright with its roses and fruit, and its glittering glass. I somehow looked at it through his eyes. His face lighted a little, as if he thought he should dine to his liking. He looked as if he were poor; but he was most carefully dressed, and I grew more and more curious about him, while I liked him better and better for the grace of his good manners, and for his charmingly bright and clever way of talking. He spoke freely of his South-American life, and of being in Europe; but there was something about him which made neither of his friends dare to ask him many questions. I could see that my cousin George was in a great hurry to know more of his history, for they had been very good friends, and he had lost sight of Mr. Whiston years before, and had been amazed when he was asked to meet him that evening. They talked a great deal about their Harvard days, and grew more and more merry with each other; but, when Mr. Whiston's face was quiet, the look of fear and melancholy was always noticeable.

When dinner was over, I went away to see one of my friends who came in just then. I could hear the gentlemen laughing together, and I stood talking in the hall some time with my friend before she went away; but at last I went back to the dining-room, for I always liked my tea there with Jack better than in the parlor. I took my chair again; and I was glad to find I did not interrupt them, of which I had a sudden fear as I entered the door.

They were talking over their army life; and my brother said, "That was the same day poor Fred Hathaway was killed, wasn't it? I never shall forget seeing his dead face. We had thrown a dozen or more men in a pile, and meant to bury them; but there was an alarm, and we had to hurry forward again, what there was left of us. I caught sight of Fred, and I remember now just how he looked. You know what yellow hair he had, and we used to call him The Pretty Saxon. I know there were one or two men in that pile still alive, and moving a little. I hardly thought of the horror of it as I went by. How used we were to such sights in those days! and now sometimes they come to me like horrid nightmares. Dunster was killed that day too. Somebody saw him fall, and I suppose he was thrown in a hurry into one of the trenches; but he was put down as missing in the reports. You know they drove us back toward night, and held that piece of cleared land and the pine-woods for two days."

"It all seems like a dream to me now," said George Sheffield. "What boys we were too! But I believe I never shall feel so old again."

"You are such comfortable people in these days," said I, "that I can't imagine you as soldiers living such a rough and cruel life as that must have been."

I happened to look up at Mr. Whiston; and to my dismay he looked paler than ever, and was uneasy. He looked over his shoulder as if he knew a ghost was standing there, and he followed something with his eyes for a moment or two in a way that gave me a little chill of fear. I looked over at Jack to know if he was watching also, and I was rejoiced when he suddenly nodded to me, and asked George Sheffield something about the cigars; and George, who had also noticed, answered him, and began to talk to me about an opera which we had both heard the evening before. I did not know whether they had chanced upon an unlucky subject, or whether Mr. Whiston was crazy; but at any rate he seemed ill at ease, and was not inclined to talk any more. He looked gloomier and more frightened than ever. I went into the library, and presently they followed me; and Mr. Whiston came to say goodnight, though, when Jack insisted that he should not go away so early,—for it was only half-past nine,—he sat down again with a half-sigh, as if it made little difference to him where he was.

"You're not well, I'm afraid, Whiston," said my brother in his most professional tone. "I think I shall have to look after you a little. By the way, are you at a hotel? I wish you would come to us for a few days. I'll drive you to Cambridge, and you know there are a good many of your old friends here in town." And I seconded this invitation, though I most devoutly hoped it would not be accepted. I had a suspicion that he would be a most uncomfortable guest.

"Thank you, Miss Ainslie," said he, with a quick, pleasant smile, that brought back my first liking for him. "You're very good, but I'm not exactly in trim for paying visits. I will come to you for to-morrow night, Ainslie, if you like. I should be glad to see you and Sheffield again—to say good-by. I am going out in the Marathon on Saturday."

Later, when he had gone, Jack and my cousin and I had a talk about this strange guest of ours. "Is he crazy?" said I to begin with; "and did you see him look at a ghost at dinner? I'm sure it was a ghost." And George Sheffield laughed; but one of us was as much puzzled as the other. "I thought at first he was melodramatic," said he; "but there's something wrong about him. Is he crazy, do you think, Jack? You're lucky in having a doctor in the house, Helen, if he does come back."

"He's not crazy," said Jack; "at least I think not. I have been watching him. But he is no doubt shattered; he may have some monomania, and I'm afraid he takes opium."

"I should urge him to spend the winter," said George serenely, "and what's the difference between having a monomania and being crazy? Couldn't he take a new fancy, and do some mischief or other some day?" But Jack only laughed, and went to a book-case; while I thought he had been very inconsiderate, and yet I wished Mr. Whiston to come again. I hoped he would tell us what it was he saw.

"Here's Bucknill and Tuke," said my brother, coming close to the drop-light, and turning over the pages; "and now you'll always know what I mean when I say 'monomania.' 'Characterized by some particular illusion impressed on the understanding, and giving rise to a partial aberration of judgment: the individual affected is rendered incapable of thinking correctly on subjects connected by the particular illusion, while in other respects he betrays no palpable disorder of the mind.' That's quoted from Prichard." And he shut the book again, and went back to put it in its place; but my cousin asked for it, and turned to another page with an air of triumph. "'An object may appear to be present before his eyes which has no existence whatever there. . . If unable to correct or recognize it when an appeal is made to reason, he is insane.' What do you think of that?" said he. "You had better be on your guard, Jack. I'm very wise just now. I have been studying up on insanity for a case of mine that's to be tried next month,—at least I devoutly hope it is."

"But tell me something about Mr. Whiston," said I. "Do you suppose he has no friends? He seems to have been wandering about the world for years."

"I remember his telling me, when we were in college, that he had no relatives except an old aunt, and a cousin, Henry Dunster, whom we spoke of to-night, who was killed in the war. Whiston was very fond of him; but I always thought Dunster was entirely unworthy his friendship. Whiston was thought to be rich. His father left him a very good property at any rate, and he was always a generous fellow. Dunster made away with a good deal, I imagine; they roomed together, and Whiston paid most of the bills. There was something weak and out-of-the-way about him then, I remember thinking, but he was a fairly good scholar, and he made a fine soldier. He was promoted fast; but you know he resigned long before the rest of us were mustered out. Had a fever, didn't he?"

"I believe so," said the judge, as his friends always called my cousin. "The snow will reach my ears by this time. I must go home. What a storm it is! No, I can't stay later. All night! no, indeed. I'll come round late to-morrow evening if I can; but it will not be likely. Now, if you had only been sensible and studied law, Jack, you wouldn't have missed the festivities: it's too bad. To tell the truth, I wish I could make some excuse, and come here instead. I'm very much excited about Whiston." And with a "good-night" to us, and a fresh cigar which he was sure the snow-storm would put out, he went away,—my lucky, easy-going cousin George Sheffield, whose cigars never did go out at inopportune times, and who never was excited about any thing. It always seemed refreshing to find in this age of hurry and dash and anxiety so calm and comfortable and satisfied a soul.

I was in doubt whether we should see any more of our sorrowful guest: but he appeared late the next afternoon; and, when I came in from my walk, I saw a much-used portmanteau being taken upstairs by Patrick, who told me that there were some flowers in the parlor that Mr. Whiston had brought. So I went in to see them, and my heart went out to the giver at once; for had he not chosen the most exquisite roses,—my favorite roses,—and more like Italy than any thing I had seen in a long day? Patrick had crammed them into exactly the wrong vase; but I thanked him for that, since it gave me a chance of handling all the beautiful heavy flowers, and making them comfortable myself, which was certainly a pleasure.

I found Mr. Whiston evidently in better spirits than he had been the night before, and I was not sorry when I found we were to be by ourselves at dinner. I had not asked any one myself, you may be sure. My brother and I have a fashion of lingering long at the table, unless I am going out for the evening; and that night he and his friend lit their cigars, and went on with their talk of old times, while I listened and read the Transcript by turns. Presently there were a few minutes of silence, and then Jack said,—

"There was a strange case brought into the city hospital to-day,—a poor young fellow who had been literally almost frightened to death. One of his fellow-clerks, who boarded with him, went into his room the night before in a horrible mask, and wrapped in a sheet, and stood near him in the moonlight, watching him until he woke. He did it for a joke, of course, and is said to be in agonies of penitence; but I'm afraid the poor victim will lose his wits entirely, if he doesn't die, which I think he will. I don't know what they can do with him. He had one fit after another. He may rally; but he looked to me as if he wouldn't hold out till morning. A nervous, slight fellow, it was a cruel thing to do. Somebody told me he belonged somewhere up in New Hampshire, and that his mother was almost entirely dependent upon him."

Mr. Whiston listened eagerly. "Poor fellow! I hope he will die," said he sadly; and then, hesitating a moment: "Do you believe in ghosts, Ainslie?"

"No," said Jack, with the least flicker of a smile as I caught his eye; "that is, I've never seen one myself. But there are very strange things that one can't explain to one's satisfaction."

"I know that the dead come back," said Mr. Whiston, speaking very low, and not looking at either of us. "John Ainslie," said he suddenly, "I never shall see you again. I'm not going to live long at any rate, and you and your sister have given me more of the old-time feeling than I have had for many a day before. It seems as if I were at home with you. I suppose you will say I am a monomaniac at the very least; but I'm going to tell you what it is that has been slowly killing me. You're a doctor, and you may put any name to it you like, and call it a disease of the brain; but Henry Dunster follows me."

Jack and I stole a glance at each other, and I felt the strongest temptation to look over my shoulder. Jack reached over, and filled Mr. Whiston's glass; and the Transcript startled me by sliding to the floor.

"I don't often speak of it now: people only laugh at the idea," said our guest, with a faint smile. "But it is most horribly real to me. It sometimes seems the only thing that is real." And this is the story he told:—

"When I was in college, you know, Henry roomed with me; and at one time we were greatly interested in what we called then superstition and foolishness. We thought ourselves very wise, and thought we could explain every thing. There was a craze among some of the students about spirit-rappings, and that sort of thing; and we went through with a good deal of nonsense, and wasted a good deal of time, in trying to ravel out mysteries, and to explain things that no mortal man has ever yet understood. One night very late we were talking, and grew much excited; and we promised each other solemnly that the one who died first would appear to the other, if such a thing were possible, and would at least warn him in a way that should be unmistakable of his death. We were half in fun and half in earnest, God forgive us! and we made that awful promise to each other. Then we went into the army, and I don't remember thinking of it once until the very night before he was killed. We were sitting together under a tree, after a hard day's fight, and Dunster said to me, laughing, 'Do you remember we promised each other, that whoever died first would appear to the other, and follow him?' I laughed,—you know how reckless we were in those days when death and dying were so horribly familiar,—and I said the same shell might kill us both, which would be a great pity. We were very merry and foolish; and I should have said Henry had been drinking, but there had been nothing to drink and hardly any thing to eat: you remember we were cut off from our supplies, and the men had very little in their haversacks. Next day the fight was hotter than ever, and we were being driven back, when I saw him toss up his hands, and fall. He must have been trodden to death at any rate. When we regained that little field beyond the woods some days afterward, they had dragged off the wounded, and buried the dead in shallow trenches. I knew Dunster was dead; and I stood on picket near a trench which was just about where he fell, and I cried in the dark like a girl. I loved Dunster. You know he was the only near relative I had in the world whom I cared any thing for, and ours wasn't a bonfire friendship. He had his faults, I know he wasn't liked in the class. He was a brilliant fellow; but I used to be afraid he might go to the bad. Do you remember that night, Ainslie? The men were so tired that they had dropped down anywhere in the mud to sleep, and there was some kind of a bird in the woods that gave a lonely, awful cry once in a while."

"I remember it," said my brother, moving uneasily in his chair, and this time I had to look behind me, there was no help for it.

"I went to the hospital soon after that," Mr. Whiston said next. "I was not badly wounded at all, but the exposure in that rainy weather played the mischief with me, and I was discharged, and, before you were mustered out, I went to South America, where a friend of mine wished me to go into business with him. I did capitally well, and I grew very strong. The climate suited me, and I used to go on those long horseback rides into the interior among the plantations that I told you about last night. My partner disliked that branch of the business far more than I did; so he left it almost wholly to me. I did not think often about Henry, though I mourned so much over his death at first, and I never was less nervous in my life.

"One evening I had just returned to Rio after an absence of several weeks, and I went to dine with some friends of mine. It was a terribly hot night, and after dinner we went out in the harbor for a sail, as the moon would be up later. There was not much wind, however; and the two boatmen took the oars, and we struck out farther, hoping to catch a breeze beyond the shipping. It was very dark, and suddenly there came by a large, heavy boat which nearly ran us down. Our men shouted angrily, and the other sailors swore; but there was no accident after all.

They seemed to be drunk, and we were all in the shadow of a brig that was lying at anchor; but, Ainslie! as that boat slid by—I was half lying in the stern of ours, and so close that I could have touched it—I saw Henry Dunster's face as plainly as I see yours now. It turned me cold for a minute, and gave me an awful shock. I told the men to give chase; and they, thinking I was angry at the carelessness, bent to their oars with a will, and overhauled them. There were two men on board,—one a negro, and the other an old gray-haired sailor,—not in the least like Henry. And I said I had been half asleep, and dreamed it was his face. But there was no mistaking him; it was the most vivid thing; it was the man himself I saw for that one horrible minute. And late the next night I was sitting in my own sleeping-room. I had reasoned myself out of the thing as well as I could, and said I was tired, and not as well as usual, and all that; and I had thought of it as calmly as possible. I sat with my back toward the window; but I was facing a mirror, and suddenly I had a strange feeling, and looked up to see in the mirror Dunster's face at the window looking in. It was staring straight at me; and I met the eyes, and that was the last I knew: I lost my senses. Only a monkey could have climbed there. There was a frail vine that clung to the stone, and in the morning there was no trace of any creature.

"And since then he follows me. I saw that haggard, wretched face of his last night when I sat here at the table; and I see him watching me if I look among a crowd of people, and, if I look back along a street, he is always coming towards me; but, when he gets near, he vanishes, and sometimes at the theatre he will be among the actors all the evening. Nobody sees him but me, but every month I see him oftener, and his face grows out of the darkness at night; and sometimes, when I talk with any one, the face will fade out, and Dunster's comes in its place. It is killing me, Ainslie. I have fought against it; I have wandered half over the world trying to get rid of it, but it is no use. For a few days in a strange place, sometimes for weeks, I did not see him at first; but I know he is always watching me now, and I see him every day."

I can give you no idea how thrilling it was to listen to this unhappy man, who seemed so pitifully cowed and broken, so helpless and hopeless. Whether there had been any thing supernatural, or whether it was merely the workings of a diseased brain, it was horribly real to him; and his life had been spoiled.

"Whiston, my dear fellow," said my brother, "I'm not going to believe in ghosts if I can possibly help it. Could you be perfectly sure that you did not see Dunster himself at first? You know he was counted among the missing only, there is no positive proof that he died, though I admit there was only a chance he was not killed outright. We never saw him buried," said Jack, with unsympathetic persistence. "I'm sorry for you; but you mustn't give way to this thing. You have thought about it until you can't forget it at all. Such cases are not uncommon: it's simply a hallucination. I'll give you proofs enough tomorrow. Have some more claret, won't you?" Jack spoke eagerly, with the kindest tone; and his guest could not help responding by a faint, dreary little smile. "Do you like music as much as ever? Suppose we go over into the parlor, and my sister will play for us; won't you, Helen?" which was asking a great deal of me just then.

And we apparently forgot all about Mr. Dunster for the rest of the evening. And, when Jack asked Mr. Whiston if he remembered a song he used to sing in college, to my delight he went at once to the piano, and sang it with a very pleasant tenor voice; and when he ended, and my brother applauded, he struck some new chords, and began to sing a little Florentine street-song, which was always a great favorite of mine. It is a sweet, piteous little song; and it bewitched me then as much as it did the very first time I had heard some boys sing it, as they went under our windows at night, when I was first in Florence years ago.

He said no more about the ghost; but later that night, when I happened to wake, I wondered if the poor man was keeping his anxious watch, and listening in a strange house to hear the hours struck one by one. He went away soon after breakfast; and, though he promised to come in again to say good-by, that was the last we saw of him, and we did not see his name on the steamer list either, so we were much puzzled, and we talked about him a great deal, and told George Sheffield the story, which he wished he had heard himself.

"Of course it is a hallucination," said Jack: "they are by no means uncommon. I can read you accounts of any number of such cases. There is a good deal about them in Griesinger's book,—the chapter called 'Elementary Disorders in Mental Disease,' Helen, if you care to look at it, or any of those books on insanity. Didn't you have Dr. Elam's 'A Physician's Problems' a while ago? He has an essay there which is very good."

"I was reading his essay on 'Moral and Criminal Epidemics,'" said I, "that was all. It's a cheerful thing too!"

"Isn't there such a thing as these visions coming before slight attacks of epilepsy?" said George. And my brother said yes; but Mr. Whiston had nothing of that kind, he had taken pains to find out. There was no hope of a cure, he feared; he was not wise in such cases. But the trouble had gone too far, there were bad symptoms, and he confesses he has hurt himself with opium during the last year or two. "He will not live long at any rate," said Jack; "and I think the sooner the end comes the better. He has a predisposition to mental disease, and he was always a frail, curious make-up. But I don't know—'There are more things in heaven and earth,' George Sheffield; and I wish you had heard him tell his story."

And we talked over some strange, unaccountable things; and each told stories which could neither be doubted nor explained. I had been readier to believe in such things since I was warned myself before the greatest sorrow I had ever known. I was by the sea; and one of my friends and I were walking slowly toward home one dark and windy evening, when suddenly we both heard a terrible low cry of fear and horror close beside us. It was hardly a cry, it was no noise that either of us had ever heard before; and we stopped for an instant, because we were too frightened to move. And the noise came again. We were in an open place, and there was nothing to be seen; but we both felt there was something there, and that the cry had some awful meaning. And it was not many days before I had reason to remember that cry; for the trouble came. I do not know what it might have been that I heard; but I knew it had the saddest meaning.

Two or three weeks after we saw Mr. Whiston, my brother came in one afternoon; and I saw he could hardly wait for some friends to go away, who were paying me a call.

"I have found poor Whiston," said he, when I joined him in the library at last: "he is at the Carney Hospital. It seems he was ill for a few days at his hotel, and the servant, who was very kind to him, advised him to go there. He insists that he is very comfortable, and that he has money enough. I wished to bring him over here at first; but I saw that it was no use, and I asked him why he didn't let me know, but he is completely wrecked; I doubt if he lives more than a day or two, he was wandering half the time I was there. He said he should be very glad if you would come to see him, and I told him I was sure you would."

I went to see him with my brother the next day, and I saw that Jack was shocked at the change that had come already. There was that peculiar, worried, anxious look in his face, that one only sees in people who are very near death, and his fingers were picking at the blanket. I do not believe he knew me; but he smiled,—he had a most beautiful smile,—and I gave him some grapes, and wished I could make him a little more comfortable. The sister came just afterward on her round, and gave him his medicine, and raised him with a strong arm, while she turned his pillow in a business-like way, and I thought what a lonely place it was to be ill and die in; and I was more glad than ever that Jack and I had a home, and were always to be together. I left Jack to stay the night, and, as I came away, I had more and more compassion for the man who was dying; yet I was glad to think so sad a life was almost over with. His days had been all winter days in this world, it seemed to me, and I hoped some wonderful, blessed spring was waiting for him in the next.

When I went over in the morning, it was cheerless enough. The rain was falling fast and the snow melting in the streets. My brother was watching for me, and came out at once. "Poor Whiston is dead," said he, as he shut the carriage-door. "He wished me to thank you for your kindness to him," and I saw the tears in Jack's eyes. "There's another star for the catalogue,—how small the class is growing! Poor fellow! I didn't know he had gone, I thought he was asleep, for we were talking together only a few minutes before. He was not at all bewildered, as you saw him yesterday."

I heard this case talked over more than once by my brother, and one or two professional friends of his who came often to the house. Nobody was ready to believe that Mr. Whiston had seen an apparition; but the truth always remained that the man's nerves were so shocked by what he believed to be the appearance of a ghost, that he had become the prey of a monomania, and had by little and little grown incapable of distinguishing between real things and the creations and projections of his own unsteady brain. *Il s'écoutait vivre*, as the French phrase has it; and, having nothing to live for but this, it was well that life was over for him. I suppose the acute disease of which he died met with little resistance, for he looked so ill when we first saw him; but it would have been sadder if he had lingered a few more years, so miserable as he was,—hardly fit either for the inside of an asylum or the outside,—to die at last without money or friends to give him the last of this world's comforts, perhaps without mind enough left to miss them.

Strangely enough, some months after this, when it was spring, my brother found Dunster at the Marine Hospital in Chelsea, where he had gone with another surgeon to see a curious operation in which he felt a great interest. He was walking through the accident ward when somebody called him from one of the cots,—a wretched-looking vagabond, whom at first he did not recognize. But it was Dunster, and he tried to put on something of his old manner, which made him seem like a wretched copy of his former self.

Jack made him give an account of himself. It seemed that he had been thrown among the dead in that battle when he was supposed to have been killed; but he had recovered his senses, and crawled from the place where he had fallen farther into the enemy's lines, and he had been sent to the rear. He had nearly died from the effects of his wounds, and it was evident that he had been very intemperate. He had drifted to New Orleans, and lead a most wretched life there; and at times he had gone to sea. My brother asked him if he was ever in Rio; and at first he denied it, and afterward confessed that he was there once, and had seen Whiston in a boat, and had dropped over the side in the dark to evade him, but when Jack questioned him about being at the window, he denied it utterly. He said his ship sailed that day. It might have been that he meant to commit a robbery, or that he really told the truth, and that it was the first of poor Whiston's illusions. Of course it was possible that Dunster might have swung himself down from the flat roof by a rope, and they might have really met at other times, it was not unlikely. But one can hardly conceive of Mr. Whiston's perfect certainty, in such a case, that the glimpse he had of his cousin's face was a supernatural vision.

My brother said, "I did not tell him what wreck and ruin he had made unconsciously of Whiston's life,—at least the part he had played in it; it would do no good, and indeed he is hardly sane, I think. It would be curious if they had both inherited from their common ancestry the mental weakness which shows itself so differently in the two lives,—Whiston's, so cowardly and shrinking and weak; and Dunster's, so horribly low and brutal. There is not much the matter with him, he had a fall on board ship. The nurse told me he was very troublesome, and had fairly insulted the chaplain, who had said a kind word to him. It is a pity that shot had not killed him; and I suppose most of the class who ever think of him will say he was a hero, and died on the field of honor."

And my brother and I talked gravely about the two men. God help us! what sin and crime may be charged to any of us who take the wrong way in life! The possibilities of wickedness and goodness in us are both unlimited. I said, how many lives must be like these which seemed such wretched failures and imperfections! One cannot help having a great pity for such men, in whom common courage, and the power of resistance, and the ordinary amount of will seem to have been wanting. Warped and incapable, or brutal and shameful, one cannot pity them enough. It is like the gnarled and worthless fruit that grows among the fair and well-rounded,—the useless growth that is despised and thrown away scornfully.

But God must always know what blighted and hindered any life or growth of His; and let us believe that He sometimes saves and pities what we have scorned and blamed.

A Late Supper

The story begins one afternoon in June just after dinner. Miss Catherine Spring was the heroine; and she lived alone in her house, which stood on the long village street in Brookton,—up in the country city people would say,—a town certainly not famous, but pleasant enough because it was on the outer edge of the mountain region, near some great hills. One never hears much about Brookton when one is away from it, but, for all that, life is as important and exciting there as it is anywhere; and it is like every other town, a miniature world, with its great people and small people, bad people and good people, its jealousy and rivalry, kindness and patient heroism.

Miss Spring had finished her dinner that day, and had washed the few dishes, and put them away. She never could get used to there being so few, because she had been one of a large family. She had put on the gray alpaca dress which she wore afternoons at home, and had taken her sewing, and sat down at one of the front windows in the sitting-room, which was shaded by a green old lilac-bush. But she did not sew as if she were much interested in the work, or were in any hurry; and presently she laid it down altogether, and tapped on the window-sill with her thimble, looking as if she were lost in not very pleasant thought. She was a very good woman, and a very pleasant woman; a good neighbor all the people would tell you; and they would add also, very comfortably left. But of late she had been somewhat troubled; to tell the truth, her money affairs had gone wrong, and just now she did not exactly know what to do. She felt more solitary than she had for a long time before. Her father, the last of the family except herself, had been dead for many years; and she had been living alone, growing more and more contented in the comfortable, prim, white house, after the first sharp grief of her loneliness had worn away into a more resigned and familiar sorrow. It is, after all, a great satisfaction to do as one pleases.

Now, as I have said, she had lost part of her already small income, and she did not know what to do. The first loss could be borne; but the second seemed to put housekeeping out of the question, and this was a dreadful thing to think of. She knew no other way of living, beside having her own house and her own fashion of doing things. If it had been possible, she would have liked to take some boarders; but summer boarders had not yet found out Brookton. Mr. Elden, the kind old lawyer who was her chief adviser, had told her to put an advertisement in one of the Boston papers, and she had done so; but it never had been answered, which was not only a disappointment but a mortification as well. Her money was not actually lost: it was the failure of a certain railway to pay its dividend, that was making her so much trouble.

Miss Spring tapped her thimble still faster on the window-sill, and thought busily. "I'm going to think it out, and settle it this afternoon," said she to herself. "I must settle it somehow, I will not live on here any longer as if I could afford it." There was a niece of hers who lived in Lowell, who was married and not at all strong. There were three children, with nobody in particular to look after them. Miss Catherine was sure this niece would like nothing better than to have her come to stay with her. She thought with satisfaction how well she could manage there, and how well her housekeeping capabilities would come into play. It had grieved her in her last visit to see the house half cared for, and she remembered the wistful way Mary had said, "How I wish I could have you here all the time, Aunt Catherine!" and at once Aunt Catherine went on to build a little castle in the air, until she had a chilly consciousness that her own house was to be shut up. She compared the attractions of Lowell and Brookton most disdainfully: the dread came over her that most elderly people feel at leaving their familiar homes and the surroundings to which they have grown used. But she bravely faced all this, and resolved to write Mary that evening, so the letter could go by the morning's mail. If Mary liked the plan, which Miss Catherine never for an instant doubted, she would stay through the early fall at any rate, and then see what was best to be done.

She took up her sewing again, and looked critically at it through her spectacles, and then went on with her stitching, feeling lighter-hearted now that the question was decided. The tall clock struck three slowly; and she said to herself how fast the last hour had gone. There was a little breeze outside which came rustling through the lilac-leaves. The wide street was left to itself, nobody had driven by since she had sat at the window. She heard some children laughing and calling to each other where they were at play in a yard not far away, and smiled in sympathy; for her heart had never grown old. The smell of the roses by the gate came blowing in sweet and fresh, and she could see the great red peonies in generous bloom on the borders each side the front walk. And, when she looked round the room, it seemed very pleasant to her, the clock ticked steadily; and the old-fashioned chairs, and the narrow high mirror with the gilt eagle at the top, the stiff faded portraits of her father and mother in their young days, the wide old brass-nailed sofa with its dim worsted-worked cushion at either end,—how comfortable it all was! and a great thrill of fondness for the room and the house came over our friend. "I didn't know I cared so much about the old place," said she. "'There's no place like home.'—I believe I never knew that meant so much before;" and she laid down her sewing again, and fell into a reverie.

In a little while she heard the click of the gate-latch; and, with the start and curiosity a village woman instinctively feels at the knowledge of somebody's coming in at the front-door, she hurried to the other front-window to take a look at her visitor through the blinds. It was only a child, and Miss Catherine did not wait for her to rap with the high and heavy knocker, but was standing in the open doorway when the little girl reached the steps.

"Come in, dear!" said Miss Catherine kindly, "did you come of an errand?"

"I wanted to ask you something," said the child, following her into the sitting-room, and taking the chair next the door with a shy smile that had something appealing about it. "I came to ask you if you want a girl this summer."

"Why, no, I never keep help," said Miss Spring. "There is a woman who comes Mondays and Tuesdays, and other days when I need her. Who is it that wants to come?"

"It's only me," said the child. "I'm small of my age; but I'm past ten, and I can work real smart about house." A great cloud of disappointment came over her face.

"Whose child are you?"

"I'm Katy Dunning, and I live with my aunt down by Sandy-river Bridge. Her girl is big enough to help round now, and she said I must find a place. She would keep me if she could," said the little girl in a grown-up, old-fashioned way; "but times are going to be dreadful hard, they say, and it takes a good deal to keep so many."

"What made you come here?" asked Miss Catherine, whose heart went out toward this hard-worked, womanly little thing. It seemed so pitiful that so young a child, who ought to be still at play, should already know about hard times, and have begun to fight the battle of life. A year ago she had thought of taking just such a girl to save steps, and for the sake of having somebody in the house; but it never could be more out of the question than now. "What made you come to me?"

"Mr. Rand, at the post-office, told aunt that perhaps you might want me: he couldn't think of anybody else."

She was such a neat-looking, well-mended child, and looked Miss Catherine in the face so honestly! She might cry a little after she was outside the gate, but not now.

"I'm really sorry," said Miss Spring; "but you see, I'm thinking about shutting my house up this summer." She would not allow to herself that it was for any longer. "But you keep up a good heart. I know a good many folks, and perhaps I can hear of a place for you. I suppose you could mind a baby, couldn't you? No: you sit still a minute!" as the child thanked her, and rose to go away; and she went out to her dining-room closet to a deep jar, and took out two of her best pound-cakes, which she made so seldom now, and saved with great care. She put these on a pretty pink-and-white china plate, and filled a mug with milk. "Here," said she, as she came back, "I want you to eat these cakes. You have walked a long ways, and it'll do you good. Sit right up to the table, and I'll spread a newspaper over the cloth."

Katy looked at her with surprise and gratitude. "I'm very much obliged," said she; and her first bite of the cake seemed the most delicious thing she had ever tasted.

Yes, I suppose bread and butter would have been quite as good for her, and much less extravagant on Miss Catherine's part; but of all the people who had praised her pound-cakes, nobody had so delighted in their goodness as this hungry little girl, who had hardly ever eaten any thing but bread all her days, and not very good bread at that.

"Don't hurry," said Miss Spring kindly, "you're a good girl, and I wish I could take you,—I declare I do." And, with a little sigh, she sat down by the window again, and took up the much-neglected sewing, looking up now and then at her happy guest. When she saw the mug was empty, and that Katy looked at it wistfully as she put it down, she took it without a word, and went to the shelf in the cellar-way where the cream-pitcher stood, and poured out every drop that was in it, afterward filling the mug to the brim with milk, for her little pitcher did not hold much. "I'll get along one night without cream in my tea," said she to herself. "That was only skim-milk she had first, and she looks hungry."

"It's real pleasant here," said Katy, "you're so good! Aunt said I could tell you, if you wanted to take me, that I don't tear my clothes, and I'm careful about the dishes. She thought I wouldn't be a bother. Would you tell the other people? I should be real glad to get a place."

"I'll tell 'em you're a good girl," said Miss Catherine; "and I'll get you a good home if I can." For she thought of her niece in Lowell, and how much trouble there was when she was there about getting a careful young girl to take care of the smallest child. Then it occurred to her that Katy was very small herself, and did not look very strong, and Mary might not hear to it; so, after Katy had gone, she began to be sorrowful again, and to wish she had promised less, and need not disappoint the little thing.

Another hour had gone, and it was four o'clock now, and in a few minutes she heard a carriage stop at the gate. She heard several voices, and was discouraged for a minute. Three people were coming in; and she was so glad when she saw it was a nephew and his wife from a town a dozen miles away, and a friend with them whom she had often seen at their house. They came in with good-natured chatter and much laughing. They had started out for a drive early after dinner, and had found the weather so pleasant that they had kept on to Brookton.

"I don't know what the folks will think," said they: "we meant to be back right away."—"Well," said the niece, "I'm so glad we found you at home; and how well you do look, Aunt Catherine! I declare, you're smarter than any of us."

"I guess she is," said her nephew, who was a great favorite. "I tell you she's the salt of the earth." And he gave her a most affectionate and resounding great kiss, and then they were all merrier than ever.

"What are you sitting down for, without laying off your bonnets?" asked the hostess. "You must stay and get supper before you ride home. I'll have it early, and there's a moon. You take the horse right round into the yard, Joseph: there's some more of that old hay in the barn; you know where to find it." And, after some persuasion, the visitors yielded, and settled themselves quietly for the rest of the afternoon. They had said, as they came over, that they were sure Aunt Catherine would ask them to stay until evening, and she always had such good suppers. Miss Stanby had never been at the house before, and only once as far as Brookton; and she seemed very pleased. She took care of her step-mother, who was very old, and a great deal crosser than there was any need of being. This little excursion would do her a world of good; and luckily her married sister happened to be at home for a day or two's visit, so she did not feel anxious about being away. She was a sharp-faced, harassed-looking little woman, who might have been pretty if she had been richer and less worried and disappointed. She was a pleasant and patient soul, and this drive and visit were more to her than a journey to Boston would be to her companions. They were well-to-do village people, comfortable and happy and unenvious as it is possible for village people, or any other people, to be.

Miss Spring was a little distracted and a bit formal for a few minutes, while she was thinking what she could get for tea; but that being settled, she gave her whole mind to enjoying the guests. She regretted the absence of the two pound-cakes Katy Dunning had eaten, but it was only for an instant. She could make out with new gingerbread, and no matter if she couldn't! It was all very pleasant and sociable: and they talked together for a while busily, telling the news and asking and answering questions; and, by and by, Joseph took his hat, saying that he must go down to the post-office to see Mr. Rand, the storekeeper. Soon after this it was time to get supper. Just as Miss Spring was going out, her niece said, "I had a letter from Lowell yesterday, from Mary."

"How is she now?" Miss Spring meant to talk over her plans a little with Joseph after supper, but was silent enough about them now.

"Her husband's oldest sister is coming to stay all summer with them. She is a widow, and has been living out West. It'll be a great help to Mary, and John sets every thing by this sister. She is a good deal older than he, and brought him up."

"It is a good thing," said Miss Catherine emphatically, and with perfect composure. "I have been thinking about Mary lately. I pitied her so when I was there. I have had half a mind to go and stay with her a while myself."

"You might have got sick going to Lowell in hot weather. Sha'n't I come out and help you, Aunt Catherine?" who said, "No indeed;" and went out to the kitchen, and dropped into a chair. "Oh, what am I going to do?" said she; for she never had felt so helpless and hopeless in her life.

The old clock gave its quick little cluck, by way of reminder that in five minutes it would be five o'clock. She had promised to have tea early; so she opened a drawer to take out a big calico apron, and went to work. Her eyes were full of tears. Poor woman! she felt as if she had come face to face with a great wall, but she bravely went to work to make the cream-tartar biscuit. Somehow she couldn't remember how much to take of any thing. She was quite confused when she tried to remember the familiar rule. It was silly!—she had made them hundreds of times, and was celebrated for her skill. Cream-tartar biscuit, and some cold bread, and some preserved plums; or was it citron-melon she meant to have?—and some of that cold meat she had for dinner, for a relish, with a bit of cheese.

She would have felt much more miserable if she had not had to hurry; and after a few minutes, when the first shock of her bad news had been dulled a little, she was herself again; and tea was nearly ready, the biscuits baking in the oven, and some molasses gingerbread beside, when she happened to remember that there was not a drop of cream in the cream-pitcher, she had given it all to poor little Katy. Joseph was very particular about having cream in his tea; so she called her niece Martha to the kitchen, and asked her to watch the oven while she went down the road to a neighbor's. She did not stop even to take her sunbonnet: it was not a great way, and shady under the elms; so away she went with the pitcher. Mrs. Hilton, the neighbor, was a generous soul, and when she heard of the unexpected company, with ready sympathy and interest she said; "Now, what did you bring such a mite of a pitcher for? Do take this one of mine. I'd just as soon you'd have the cream as not. I don't calculate to make any butter this week, and it'll be well to have it to eat with your preserves. It's nice and sweet as ever you saw."

"I'm sure you are kind," said Miss Spring; and with a word or two more she went hurrying home. As I have said, it was not far; but the railroad came between, and our friend had to cross the track. It seemed very provoking that a long train should be standing across the road. It seemed to be waiting for something; an accident might have happened, for the station was a little distance back.

Miss Catherine waited in great anxiety; she could not afford to waste a minute. She would have to cross an impossible culvert in going around the train either way. She saw some passengers or brakemen walking about on the other side, and with great heroism mounted the high step of the platform with the full intention of going down the other side, when, to her horror, the train suddenly moved. She screamed, "Stop! stop!" but nobody saw her, and nobody heard her; and off she went, cream-pitcher and all, without a bit of a bonnet. It was simply awful.

The car behind her was the smoking-car, and the one on which she stood happened to be the Pullman. She was dizzy, and did not dare to stay where she was; so she opened the door and went in. There was a young lady standing in the passage-way, getting a drink of water for some one in a dainty little tumbler; and she looked over her shoulder, thinking Miss Spring was the conductor, to whom she wished to speak; and she smiled, for who could help it?

"I'm carried off," said poor Aunt Catherine hysterically. "I had company come to tea unexpectedly, and I was all out of cream, and I went out to Mrs. Hilton's, and I was in a great hurry to get back, and there seemed no sign in the world of the cars starting. I wish we never had sold our land for the track! Oh! what shall I do? I'm a mile from home already; they'll be frightened to death, and I wanted to have supper early for them, so they could start for home; it's a long ride. And the biscuit ought to be eaten hot. Dear me! they'll be so worried!"

"I'm very sorry, indeed," said the young lady, who was quivering with laughter in spite of her heartfelt sympathy for such a calamity as this. "I suppose you will have to go on to the next station; is it very far?"

"Half an hour," said Miss Spring despairingly; "and the down train doesn't get into Brookton until seven; and I haven't a cent of money with me, either. I shall be crazy! I don't see why I didn't get off; but it took all my wits away the minute I found I was going."

"I'm so glad you didn't try to get off," said the girl gravely: "you might have been terribly hurt. Won't you come into the compartment just here with my aunt and me? She is an invalid, and we are all by ourselves; you need not see any one else. Let me take your pitcher." And Miss Spring, glad to find so kind a friend in such an emergency, followed her.

There were two sofas running the length of the compartment, and on one of these was lying a most kind and refined-looking woman, with gray hair and the sweetest eyes. Poor Aunt Catherine somehow felt comforted at once; and when this new friend looked up wonderingly, and her niece tried to keep from even smiling while she told the story discreetly, she began to laugh at herself heartily.

"I know you want to laugh, dear," said she. "It's ridiculous, only I'm so afraid they'll be worried about me at home. If anybody had only seen me as I rode off, and could tell them!"

Miss Ashton had not laughed so much in a long time, the fun of the thing outweighed the misery, and they were all very merry for a few minutes. There was something straightforward and homelike and pleasant in Miss Catherine's face, and the other travellers liked her at once, as she did them. They were going to a town nearer the mountains for the summer. Miss Ashton was just getting over a severe illness; and

SARAH ORNE JEWETT

they asked about the place to which they were bound, but Miss Spring could tell them little about it.

"The country is beautiful around here, isn't it?" said Alice West, when there was a pause: the shadows were growing long, and the sun was almost ready to go down among the hills. "Brookton! didn't you notice an advertisement of some one who wanted boarders there, aunty? You thought it was hardly near enough to the mountains, didn't you? but this is beautiful."

"Why, that was my notice," said Miss Spring; and then she stopped, and flushed a little. I believe, if she had thought a moment, she would not have spoken; but Miss Ashton saw the hesitation and the flush.

"I wish I were going to spend the summer with you," said she by and by, in her frank, pleasant way. And Miss Catherine said, "I wish you were," and sighed quietly; she felt wonderfully at home with these strangers, and, in spite of her annoyance when she thought of her guests, she was enjoying herself. "I live all alone," she said once, in speaking of something else; and, if she had been alone with Miss Ashton, I think she would have told her something of her troubles, of which we know her heart was very full. Everybody found it easy to talk to Miss Ashton, but there was the niece; and Miss Catherine, like most elderly women of strong character who live alone, was used to keeping her affairs to herself, and felt a certain pride in being uncommunicative.

When the conductor looked in, with surprise at seeing the new passenger, Alice West asked him the fare to Hillsfield, the next station; and, after paying him, gave as much money to Miss Spring, who took it reluctantly, though there was nothing else to be done.

"I'm sure I don't know how to thank you," said she; "but you must tell me how to direct to you and I will send the money back tomorrow."

"No, indeed!" said the girl: but Miss Spring looked unhappy; and Miss Ashton, with truer kindness, gave her the direction, saying,—

"Please tell us how you found your friends at home; because Alice and I will wish very much to know what they thought."

"You have been so kind; I sha'n't forget it," said Miss Catherine, with a little shake in her voice that was not made by the cars.

Alice had taken from her travelling-bag a little white hood which she had seen in a drawer that morning after her trunk was locked and strapped, and had put it over Miss Catherine's head. It was very becoming, and it did not look at all unsuitable for an elderly woman to wear in the evening, just from one station to the next. And she was going to wrap the cream-pitcher in some paper, when Miss Catherine said softly,—

"Does your aunty care any thing about cream?"

"She likes it dearly," said the girl, looking so much pleased. "I had half a mind to ask you if you could spare just a little;" and Miss Ashton's little tumbler was at once delightedly filled to the very brim.

Its owner said she had not tasted any thing so delicious in a long time; and would not Miss Spring take some little biscuit and some grapes to eat while she waited in the station? Yes, indeed: they had more than they wanted, and she must not forget it was tea-time already. Alice would wrap some up for her in a paper.

And at last they shook hands most cordially, and were so sorry to say good-by.

"I never shall forget your kindness as long as I live," said Miss Catherine; and Alice helped her off the car, and nodded good-by as it started.

"I wish with all my heart we could board with that dear good soul this summer," said Miss Ashton, "and I believe she has been dreadfully grieved because her advertisement was not answered; perhaps it may be yet. She looked sad and worried, and it was something besides this mishap. What a kind face she had! I wish we knew more about her. I'm so glad we happened to be just here, and that she didn't have to go into the car."

"Yes," said Alice; "but, aunty, I think it was the funniest thing I ever saw in my life, when she appeared to me with that horror-stricken face and her cream-pitcher."

And Miss Catherine, as she seated herself in the little station to wait for the down-train, said to herself, "God bless them! how good they were! How I should have hated to go into the car with all the people, and be stared at and made fun of." They had been so courteous and simple and kind: why are there not more such people in the world? And she thought about them, and ate her crackers and the hot-house grapes, and was very comfortable. It might have been such a disagreeable experience, yet she had really enjoyed herself. It did not seem long before she again took her seat in the cars, with the cream-pitcher respectably disguised in white paper, and herself looking well enough in the soft little white hood, with its corner just in the middle of her gray hair over her forehead; she paid her fare as if her pocket were full of money, and watched the other people in the car; and by the time she reached home she was her own composed and reliable self again.

There had been a great excitement at her house. The biscuit were done and the gingerbread; and the niece took them out of the oven, and thought her aunt was gone a good while, and went back to the sitting-room. After a few minutes she went to the front-gate to look down the street. Miss Stanby joined her; and they stood watching until Joseph Spring came hurrying back, thinking he was late, and ready with his apologies, when they told him how long Miss Catherine had been gone.

"She's stopped for something or other: they're always asking her advice about things," said he carelessly. "She will be along soon." And then they went into the house; and nobody said much, and the tall clock ticked louder and louder; and Joseph began to whistle and drum with his fingers, meaning to show his unconcern, but in reality betraying the opposite feeling.

"You don't suppose she's sick, do you?" asked Miss Stanby timidly.

"More likely somebody else is," said Mr. Spring. "Did you say she had gone to Mrs. Hilton's, Martha? I'll walk down there, and see what the matter is."

"I wish you would," said his wife. "It's after six o'clock."

"Hasn't got home yet!" said Mrs. Hilton in dismay. "Why, what can have become of her? She came in before half-past five, in a great hurry; and she left her pitcher here on the table. I suppose she forgot it. I lent her mine, because it was bigger. There's no house between but the Donalds', and they're all off at his mother's funeral to Lancaster. You don't suppose the cars run over her?"

"I don't know," said Miss Spring's nephew, in real trouble by this time.

They went out together, and looked everywhere along the road, apologizing to each other as they did so. They went up and down the railroad for some little distance, and it was a great relief not to find her there. Joseph asked some men if they had seen his aunt; and when they said no, wonderingly, and expected an explanation, he did not give it, he hardly knew why. They went to the house beyond Miss Catherine's, though Martha and Miss Stanby were sure she had not gone by. They looked in the barn even: they went out into the garden and through the house, for she might possibly have come in without being seen; but she had apparently disappeared from the face of the earth.

It had seemed so foolish at first to tell the neighbors; but by seven o'clock, or nearly that, Martha Spring said decisively, "She cannot have gone far unless she has been carried off. I think you had better get some men, and have a regular hunt for her before it gets any darker. I'm not going home to-night until we find her." And they owned to each other that it was a very serious and frightful thing. Miss Stanby looked most concerned and apprehensive of the three, and suggested what had been uppermost in her mind all the time,—that it would be so awful if poor Miss Spring had been murdered, or could she have killed herself? There was something so uncharacteristic in the idea of Miss Catherine's committing suicide, that for a moment her nephew could not resist a smile; but he was grave enough again directly, for it might be true, after all, and he remembered with a thrill of horror that old Mr. Elden, the lawyer, had told him in confidence, that Miss Spring was somewhat pinched for money,—that her affairs were in rather a bad way, and perhaps he had better talk with her, as he himself did not like to have all the responsibility of advising her.

"Poor old lady!" thought Joseph Spring, who was a tender-hearted man. "She looked to-day as if she felt bad about something. She has grown old this last year, that's a fact!" It seemed to him as if she were in truth dead already. "You had better look all over the house," said he to his wife. "Did you look in the garret?" He remembered the story that his great-grandfather had been found hanging there, and could not have gone to the garret himself to save his life.

He went hurrying out of the house, determined now to make the disappearance public. He would go to the depot, there were always some men there at this time. The church-bell began to ring for Wednesday-evening meeting, and she had always gone so regularly; he would hurry back there, and tell the people as they came. The train went by slowly to stop at the station, it was a little behind time. He hurried on, looking down as he walked. To tell the truth, he was thinking about the funeral, and suddenly he heard a familiar voice say,—

"Well, Joseph! I suppose you thought I was lost!"

"Heavens and earth, Aunt Catherine! Where have you been?" And he caught her by the shoulder, and felt suddenly like crying and laughing together. "I never had any thing come over me so in all my life," said he to his wife and Miss Stanby, as they went home later that evening. "I declare, it took the wits right out of me."

Miss Catherine looked brighter than she had that afternoon, the excitement really had done her good; she told her adventure as they hurried home together. When they reached the house Martha Spring and Miss Stanby kissed her, and cried as if their hearts would break. Joseph looked out of the window a few minutes, and then announced that he would go out and see to the horse.

The tears were soon over with; and, as soon as it seemed decent, Mrs. Martha said, "Aunt Catherine, do tell me where you got that pretty hood! I wish I had seen it when I first got here, to take the pattern. Isn't it a new stitch?"

"Dear me! haven't I taken it off?" said Miss Catherine. "Well, you must excuse me if I am scatter-witted. I feel as if I had been gone a week."

They had supper directly—that very late supper! They were all as hungry as hunters, even poor little Miss Stanby; and the re-action from such suspense made the guests merry enough, while, as was often said, Miss Catherine was always good company. The cream-tartar biscuits were none the less good for being cold. Joseph hadn't eaten such gingerbread since he was there before; and the tea was made fresh over a dry-shingle fire, which blazes in a minute, as every one knows. There were more than enough pound-cakes; and Martha asked all over again how Miss Catherine made her preserves, for somehow hers were never so good; while Miss Catherine meekly said that she had not had such good luck as usual with the last she made.

At last they drove off down the road. The moon had come up, and was shining through the trees. It was so cool and fresh and bright an evening, with a little yellow still lingering in the west after the sunset! The guests went away very happy and light-hearted, for it seemed as if they had been spared a terrible sorrow.

"I saw the prettiest little old-fashioned table up in the garret," said Mrs. Martha. "It only needs fixing up a little. I mean to ask your Aunt Catherine if I can't have it when I go over again."

"No, you won't," said her husband, with more authority than was usual with him.

Miss Catherine stood watching at the gate until they were out of sight. "I must settle down," said she. "I feel as if it had been a wedding or a funeral or something; and I declare if it isn't Wednesday evening, and what will they think has become of me at meeting?" though she could have trusted Mrs. Hilton to spread the story far and wide—by which you must not suppose that good Mrs. Hilton was a naughty gossip.

The next morning Miss Catherine waked up even more heavy-hearted than she had been the day before. I suppose she was tired after the unusual excitement. She wished she had talked to Joseph, she must talk with somebody. She wished she had not been such a fool as to get on those cars, for she was sure she never should hear the last of the joke; and, after the morning work was done, she sat down in the sitting-room with the clock ticking mockingly, and that intolerable feeling of despair and disgust came over her; there is nothing much harder to bear than that, if you know what it is I am sure you will pity her.

The afternoon seemed very long. It rained; and nobody came in until the evening, when Mrs. Hilton's boy came with a letter. Miss Catherine had been to the post-office just before dinner, to send the money to Miss Ashton; and this surprised her very much. "It must have come by the seven-o'clock train," said she. "I never get letters from that way;" and she took it to the window, and looked curiously at the address, and at last she opened it. It was a pretty letter to look at, and it proved a pleasant one to read. It was from Alice West, Miss Ashton's niece; and Miss Catherine read it slowly, and felt as if she were in a dream.

My Dear Miss Spring,

My aunt, Miss Ashton, wishes me to write to you, to ask if it would be convenient for you to take us to board. We are very much disappointed here, and are glad we did not positively engage our rooms until we had seen them. It is a very damp house, and I am sure my aunt ought not to stay, and would be uncomfortable in many ways. We should like two rooms close to each other, and we were each to pay ten dollars a week here, but are perfectly willing to pay more than that. We are almost certain that we shall like your house; but perhaps it will be the better way for me to come down and see you, and then I can make all the arrangements. If Brookton suits my aunt, we may wish to stay as late as October; and should you mind if one of my friends comes to stay with us by and by? She would share my room. If you will write me to-morrow morning, and if you think you can take us, I will go down in the early afternoon train.

"We hope you reached home all right, and that your friends were not much worried. We begin to think that your adventure was a fortunate thing for us. With kind regards from us both,

Yours sincerely,
Alice West

SARAH ORNE JEWETT

Did you ever know any thing more fortunate than this? Poor Miss Catherine sat down and cried about it; and the cat came and rubbed against her foot, and purred sympathizingly, and was taken up and wept over, which I believe had never happened to her before. Of all people, who could be pleasanter boarders than these? They had won her heart in the half-hour she had already spent with them. She had wished then that they were coming to her: it would be such a pleasure to make them comfortable. And twenty dollars a week,—that would surely be more than enough for them all to live upon with what she had beside. And there was Katy, who could save so many steps, and could wait on Miss Ashton; she would have the child come at once. She could have Mrs. Brown come every day for a while, beside Mondays and Tuesdays; and how glad she would be of the extra pay! Miss Catherine even went up stairs in the late June twilight, to look at the two familiar front-chambers, with only the small square hall separating them. They looked so pleasant, and were so airy and of such good size, they could not help being suited. She patted the pillow of her best bed affectionately, and thought with pride that they would find no fault with her way of cooking, and her house never was damp; there was not a better house in Brookton. Life had rarely looked brighter to Miss Catherine than it did that night.

Alice West came down the next afternoon, and found the house and the rooms and Miss Catherine herself were all exactly what wise Miss Ashton had said they would be. And the two boarders thought themselves lucky to have found such a pleasant house for the summer; they were so considerate, and became favorites with many people beside their hostess. They brought a great deal of pleasure and good-will to sober little Brookton, as two cultivated, thoughtful, helpful women may make any place pleasanter if they choose. Miss Ashton is a help and a comfort and a pleasure wherever she goes, while Alice West is learning to be like her more and more every year. Miss Catherine remembered sometimes with great thankfulness, that it was the loss of her money for a while that had brought her these friends. Katy Dunning was so happy to go to live at Miss Spring's after all, and did her very best,—a patient, steady, willing little creature she was! and I am sure she never had had so many good times in her life as she did that summer.

I might tell you so much more about these people, but a story must end somewhere. You may hope that Miss Catherine's fortunes bettered, and that she never will have to give up her home; that she can keep Katy all the time; that Miss Ashton will come back to Brookton the next year, and the next.

I am sure you will think, in reading all this, just what I have thought as I told it,—and what Miss Catherine herself felt,—that it was such a wonderfully linked-together chain. All the time she thought she was going wrong, that it was a series of mistakes. "I never will be so miserable again," said she. "It was all ordered for the best; and may the Lord forgive me for doubting his care and goodness as I did that day!" It went straight to her heart the next Sunday, when the old minister said in his sermon, "Dear friends, do not let us forget what the Psalmist says, that the steps of a good man are ordered by the Lord. He plans the way we go; and so let us always try to see what he means in sending us this way or that. Do not let us go astray from wilfulness, or blame him for the work he gives us to do, or the burdens he gives us to carry, since he knows best."

So often, in looking back, we find that what seemed the unluckiest day of the week really proved most fortunate, and what we called bad luck proved just the other thing. We trace out the good results of what we thought must make every thing go wrong: we say, "If it had not been for this or that, I should have missed and lost so much." I once happened to open a book of sermons, and to see the title of one, "Every Man's Life a Plan of God." I did not read the sermon itself, and have never seen the book again; but I have thought of it a great many times. Since it is true that our lives are planned with the greatest love and wisdom, must it not be that our sorrows and hindrances come just from our taking things wrong?

And here, for the last of the story, is a verse that Robert Browning wrote, that Miss Ashton said one morning, and Miss Catherine liked:—

"Grow old along with me!
The best is yet to be,
The last of life, for which the first was made:
Our times are in His hand
Who saith 'A whole I planned,
Youth shows but half; trust God: see all, nor be afraid!'"

Mr. Bruce

L ast summer (said Aunt Mary), while you were with your father in Canada, I met for the first time Miss Margaret Tennant of Boston, whom I had for years a great desire to see and know. My dear friend, Anne Langdon, has had from her girlhood two very intimate friends; and Miss Tennant is one, and I the other. Though we each had known the other through Anne, we had never seen each other before.

I was at the mountains, and upon our being introduced we became very good friends immediately; and, from at first holding complimentary and interesting conversations concerning Anne in the hotel parlor, we came to taking long walks, and spending the most of our time together; and now we are as fond of each other as possible. When we parted in September, I had promised to visit her at her house in Boston in the winter; and, when she was ready for it, I was too.

To my great delight, I found Anne there; and we three old maiden ladies enjoyed ourselves quite as well as if we were your age, my dear, with the world before us. Miss Margaret Tennant certainly keeps house most delightfully.

She lives alone in the old Tennant house, in a pleasant street; and I think most of the Tennants, for a dozen generations back, must have been maiden ladies with exquisite taste and deep purses, just like herself; for every thing there is perfect of its kind, and its kind the right kind. Then she is such a popular person: it is charming to see the delight her friends have in her. For one thing, all the young ladies of her acquaintance—not to mention her nieces, who seem to bow down and worship her—are her devoted friends; and she often gives them dinners and tea parties, takes them to plays and concerts, matronizes them in the summer, takes them to drive in her handsome carriages, and is the repository of all their joys and sorrows, and, I have no doubt, knows them better than their fathers and mothers do, and has nearly as much influence over them. Elly, my dear, I wish you were one of the clan; for I'm afraid, between your careless papa and your wicked aunty, you haven't had the most irreproachable bringing up! But, she is coming to visit me in June, and we'll see what she can do for you!

One night, while I was there, we were just home from a charming dinner-party at the house of her sister, Mrs. Bruce; and, as it was a very stormy night, we had come away early. Not being in the least tired, we sat ourselves down in our accustomed easy-chairs before the fire, for a talk, and were lazily making plans for the morrow; Miss Tennant telling us she should have the eight young ladies whom she knew best; the Quadrille as she calls them; to dine with us. I must tell you about that party some day, Elly. It was the nicest affair in its way I ever saw, and the girls were all such dear ones! I spoke of the company we had just left, and of my admiration of the Bruce family in general, and Mrs. Bruce in particular, and of my enjoyment of the evening.

"Yes," said Margaret, "I think Kitty is quite as young as her two daughters, and at their age she was more brilliant than either." She stopped talking for a moment, and then said, "Girls, are you in a hurry for bed?" (Elly! you ought to be ashamed of yourself for laughing! Just as if Anne Langdon and I were not as young as you and Nelly Cameron. There's no difference, sometimes, if we are fifty, and you twenty!)

We were not in a hurry, and told her so.

"Then," said Margaret, "I will tell you a story. Anne knows it, or used to; but I doubt if she has thought of it these dozen years, and I do not think she will mind hearing it again. It is about Kitty and Mr. Bruce, and their first meeting; also divers singular misunderstandings which followed, finally ending in their peaceful wedding in this very room."

Anne laughed; and I settled myself contentedly in my chair, for I had already found out that Miss Tennant possesses the art of telling a story capitally.

"Kitty Bruce is three years older than I," said Margaret,—"though I dare say you do not believe me,—and consequently, at the time I was fifteen she was eighteen; and whereas I was in my first year at boarding-school, she was about finishing. I was at Mrs. Walkintwo's, where you and I met, Anne; and that, as you know, was a quiet place, where we were taught history and arithmetic, and the other 'solids,' and from which she had graduated the year before, and gone to Madame Riche's to acquire the extras and be 'finished.' Her beauty was very striking, and she was quite as entertaining and agreeable as she is now,—very witty and original, with the kindest heart in the world, and enjoying life to the utmost. In the Easter vacation of that year we were at home together; and one morning I was sitting with her in her chamber, and she was confiding to me some of the state secrets of her room at school, to my inexpressible delight, for it was my great ambition to be intimate with Kitty; and, you know, that elder sisters are often strangely blind to the virtues of the younger.

"Mamma came in in the midst of it, with her usually cheerful face exceedingly clouded, so much so that both of us immediately asked what had happened.

"'Happened!' said poor mamma, sitting down disconsolately on Kitty's bed, and helping herself, by way of relief, from a box of candy which lay there. 'I'm sure I don't know what I'm to do. Your father has just sent me a note from the office, saying he has invited four gentlemen to dine, and wishes to have every thing as nice as possible. I can send John for the dinner; and, of course, I don't mind that part of it, for there is time enough and to spare, and Peggy never fails me; but you know Hannah is away; and this morning a small Irish boy came for Ann, saying his sister is sick and she went away with him. About an hour ago another little wretch came to say she was obliged to go to Salem with the sister, and would be back to breakfast. Now, children, what shall I do for some one to wait on the table?'

"Kitty and I were as much posed as mamma. John, our coachman, was an immense Englishman, and perfectly unavailable as to taking upon himself any of Ann's duties save waiting upon the door. His daughter, who had been our nurse and was at that time seamstress, might have done very well, but she was away at Portsmouth; and as for Peggy, our dear old black cook, though I never knew any one to equal her in her realm, the kitchen, she had no idea of any thing out of it, and never had done any thing of this kind. It was raining in torrents, and none of us could go out; and we sat and looked at each other.

"Suddenly Kitty clapped her hands. 'Mamma,' said she, 'read us their names again.'

"So mamma read the names of two gentlemen from South America, and one from New Orleans, and that of Mr. Philip Bruce of London.

"'All perfect strangers except to papa,' said Kitty joyfully; 'and they're interested in that South-American business of his, and are all on their way there very likely; and we shall never see them again.'

"'Well, child, what has all this to do with Ann's being gone?'

"'I'll tell you, mamma: I have the jolliest plan, and it will be such fun! I shall be so disappointed if you say no to me. It isn't the least harm, and I know it will make no trouble. Just let me wear one of Ann's white aprons and look stupid, you call me Katherine, and I'll wait on the table as well as she could. No one ever notices the servants, and I'm not like you or papa or Margaret. You can turn my portrait to the wall in the drawing-room, and they'll think it's somebody that is disinherited. Those gentlemen haven't the least particle of information concerning papa's family; they may be possessed of the delusion that he is a bachelor in lodgings, for all we know; and if any thing is said about your children, tell them that your sons are in college and your eldest daughter with a friend. Of course I shall be, whether I am with Peggy in the kitchen or standing behind you. Oh! I'd like it so much better than sitting at the table; and Peggy will never tell. Who will be the wiser?'

"Mamma at first, though very much amused, shook her head, and said it was too foolish to be thought of; we could explain our troubles to the gentlemen, and get on as best we could; but Kate would not give up. Mamma gave some very good reasons; what should we do without Kitty to help entertain them? And any one,—though she knew it wouldn't be considered proper conduct in a mother to make such a remark,—any one would know Kate was not a servant. Papa, too, would want her to sing for them in the evening (for, though her voice is wonderfully sweet now, then she sang like a bird; and we were all very proud of the girl, as well we might be).

"But she upset all mamma's arguments, asking her how in the world she entertained so much company unaided, during the years she was unable to appear on account of extreme youth. She was charmed to hear her say she was too good looking; but as to her being wanted to sing, just see if the whole five didn't go directly to the library, and if the waste-paper basket wasn't filled with papers covered with figures in the morning!

"And so the end was, that mamma very reluctantly yielded to our teasing. Peggy, to whom the secret was instantly confided, nearly went into fits with laughing; and the more we all thought of it the more we were amused. Kitty suggested our total discomfiture in case papa brought home some one who knew her. I suggested, that, if it were any one we were intimate with, we take them into the secret, for I wished to see how Kate would carry it out; and if it were not, we might— and thereby I nearly ruined the whole affair—send for the 'lending' of Mrs. Duncan's Mary,—Mrs. Duncan being a great friend of ours, who lived only a door or two away. Such a pull as Kitty gave my dress when I mentioned it!

"However, in due season papa appeared with the four strangers, who had been at the office with him all day, and, luckily, no one with them.

He was duly made acquainted with the programme for the evening; and finding the plans all settled, and Kitty's heart evidently set upon them, he made but little opposition, considering the disappointment it probably was to him not to show his uncommonly nice little daughter. We three could hardly conceal our amusement when Kate entered the drawing-room to announce dinner; and it was made the harder for us by the queer little Irish brogue she had assumed for the occasion. The guests—one in particular—could evidently not account for so striking a display of beauty and grace in so humble a position.

"The dinner went off capitally. Kitty was perfection; and the only way I could see that she betrayed herself was in having, for a moment or two, the most interested expression during a conversation we were all very much interested in. She told me afterward that she came very near giving her opinion,—and I know it would have been very sensible and original,—in the most decided manner. Wouldn't it have been shocking?

"We sat a much longer time than usual. The three gentlemen from the South were middle-aged, and evidently absorbed in business; but the Englishman was not over thirty, and as handsome and agreeable as possible. He watched Kitty as often as he dared, to our great amusement; and once, as she left the room, seemed on the point of asking us about her. My dears, what could mamma have said?

"Papa was overflowing with fun, and enjoyed it all very much. I could see he was nearly choking sometimes at Kitty's unnecessary 'Yis, sur-rs.' She never passed me a plate without giving me a poke; and, I dare say, reminded papa and mamma of her existence in the same way.

"As she had prophesied, they excused themselves after dinner, and went to the library,—all but Mr. Bruce, who had no interest in South America. He had an engagement, and so left us in the course of half an hour. Conceive our amusement, when, just after we left the table, Kitty entered with a note on a waiter, and a message purporting to be from Miss Harriet Wolfe, to the effect that she would call for mamma to go to an afternoon concert the next day. I was just leaving the room as she entered; and I can tell you I hurried a bit after that; and, as I looked around at mamma to see how she bore it, she was holding a fan before her face, in a perfect convulsion of laughter; and there stood that wicked Kate, with her hands folded, waiting solemnly for the answer. Poor Miss Wolfe had died some years before, and had been stone-deaf at that! How mamma gave the answer, or excused her amusement, I have forgotten. Kitty did it, as she said then, for a grand finale to her masquerading; but as she says now, and I firmly believed at the time, for a parting look at the Englishman.

"He went away, and Kitty came into the parlor, and we had a great laugh over our dinner-party; and the next day it was told to an admiring audience of three,—grandmamma and my two aunts; but I think the story never went any farther, as we did not even dare to tell my brothers. Ann probably wonders to this day who took her place.

"The next Monday we went back to our two boarding-schools, and after a while we forgot the whole affair. Kitty finished school with high honors in July, and 'came out' in November, and was a great belle in Boston all that winter. I, in durance vile at Mrs. Walkintwo's, read her journal-letters to a select circle of friends; and they were a green spot in our so-considered desert of life.

"Towards the last of the winter, papa's sister, for whom Kate was named, and who was very fond of her, sent for my sister to come to her for a visit of a few weeks during my uncle's absence. She wrote she would not have to suspend her pleasure in the least, as there had never been more gayety in Baltimore than at that time; and some young friends of Kitty's had that very day come from Europe, which was a great inducement. Baltimore was a kind of paradise to her, and her friends there were very dear ones. Her room-mate at Madame Riche's, who was her very best friend, lived quite near my uncle Hunter's, and she had not seen her for months. Besides, Boston was getting dull, and she was tired, and Baltimore air always made her well. So it was settled, and Kitty went.

"Papa carried her on; and for the first week she had a cold, and was not out of the house. However, her letters were very happy ones; the contents being mostly abstracts of conversations between herself and the dear Alice Thornton, and bits of Baltimore gossip, in which I wasn't particularly interested. But the cold got better, and her letters grew rather shorter as she got farther into the round of parties and pleasure.

"Finally there came a very thick letter, and there was something new on the stage. She wrote to me somewhat after this fashion, while staying with Miss Thornton:—

"'You're not to tell this, Margie; but I'm getting involved in what seems to be a mystery. Ever since I've been here, the girls have talked to me of the most charming gentleman ever seen in Baltimore, and they all declared I must be introduced; so at last I got up quite a curiosity.

They said he was an Englishman, very rich, and so handsome! why! if one were to believe their stories, he might be carried about for a show! He was said to be very reserved, and to pay very little attention to any of the young ladies. He knows Mr. Thornton, Alice's father; and they are good friends, so Alice has seen a good deal of him, and he has been more polite to her than to any one else.

"'She had told him of me, and he seemed quite anxious to know me. She had promised to present him the very first chance, and that was last night at her party.

"'I wish I had time to tell you about it. Every one says it was one of the most delightful ones ever given in Baltimore, and I did enjoy it wonderfully. But do let me tell you about the Englishman. It was about eleven before he came, and every thing was at its height. I was dancing with Mr. Dent; and the moment I stopped, up came Alice, with the most elegant-looking man I ever saw; and the strangest thing is, that I think now, and thought then, I have seen him somewhere before. He watched me intently as he crossed the room, and asked Alice, as she has told me to-day, who I was; and when she said, "That is Kitty Tennant," he looked as pleased as Punch. Don't tell mamma,' said Kitty. I keep wondering where it is I have met him; but I know I cannot have, for they say he is just from England. But you don't know how queerly he acted. All at once he looked as puzzled as could be; and by the time he was close to me he stared in the queerest way; and when Alice introduced us, he bowed, and said, "Haven't we met before, Miss Tennant?" I said, "I think so;" and said I wished he would help me remember, for I was very certain I had seen him.

"'Suddenly it seemed to flash into his mind; and he said to himself, "It couldn't be." But I heard him; and after that he was a perfect icicle; and I didn't have the courage to ask him any questions, for I knew it was something horrid by his looks. He evidently mistakes me for some one, and it is so queer that I firmly believe I have seen him. He went away from me in a very few minutes, and staid only a half-hour or so, avoiding Alice all the time. I had promised all the dances, and was desperately' busy all night, having such a good time that I quite forgot this unpleasant affair. Alice came to me after the people were gone away, and said, "Kate Tennant, what did you say to the poor man?" And she seemed so utterly astonished when I told her what had happened. She cannot account for it any more than I can, and says it is as unlike him as possible. I don't know whether I have told you his name: it is Bruce.'"

When Miss Tennant reached this point in her story, I laughed heartily (said Aunt Mary); and Anne and she laughed with me. "Why in the world didn't she know him," said I: "I should have thought the circumstances would have made her remember him always."

Miss Tennant said, "Indeed, I should have thought so too. I know I should have recognized him myself if I had seen him; but Kitty was always the very worst person in the world to remember people, and it had happened a year before nearly. We always had a great many guests.

"When I answered her letter, I said nothing about him; for I must confess that I did not recollect that the gentleman who stared so at Kitty the night she played waiter was Mr. Bruce of London; and, indeed, I didn't feel particularly interested; and my reply was probably filled as usual with an account of the exciting things that had happened to me at the school from which I so earnestly longed for deliverance.

"Kitty wrote me very often; and once in a while she mentioned this strange Mr. Bruce, and finally it occurred to me that my sister was getting very much interested in him; and as I had a woeful dread of losing her, I expostulated with her concerning the foolishness of caring any thing for a man who had treated her in so uncourteous a way, and I laughed at her.

"For some time after that she did not allude to him, and I had nearly forgotten him. At last there came a letter in which Kitty said, "I must tell you more of Mr. Bruce, if you *are* tired to death hearing of him; for it is really a perfect mystery. I have seen him at a number of parties, watching me in the most earnest way, as if he enjoyed it and still was rather ashamed. But when we meet he is just as cool and distant as possible. Alice and I have missed his calls; and all the way he has betrayed the slightest interest in me to any one else is that he met a Miss Burt, who has only lived here a short time, and to whom he had been presented a night or two before. He asked her incidentally if she knew Miss Alice Thornton; and, when she said she did a very little, he asked who the young lady was visiting her. Miss Burt said she never had seen her, but some one had told her it was a young lady Miss Thornton had met at boarding-school. "Then she has never been here before?" said he. And Miss Burt thought not, indeed was quite sure, as she never had heard of me. Isn't it a pity he didn't ask some one who could tell him all about me?—and then he could know whether he had met me, of course.'

"Now Kitty, in that same letter, confessed to me that she liked Mr. Bruce better than any one she had ever seen, which alarmed me so much that I remember I wrote her the most shocking scolding."

And here Miss Tennant was silent for a little while, and, when she spoke, said,—

"I see by your faces you're quite interested; and I think the rest of the story cannot be better told than by my reading you some of the letters Kitty wrote to me at the time. I'd like to look them over myself; and, if you are not in the least sleepy, I will go up to my room and get them."

In a few minutes she returned; and after making the gas and fire a little brighter, and taking an observation on the state of the weather, she began to read:—

Baltimore, Friday.

"My forlorn young sister, are you mourning over the inconstancy of woman in general, and your sister Kitty in particular? I own up to being very naughty, and on my knees I ask your pardon for not having written all these days. I cannot tell you, as you invariably do me, that I have had nothing to write; for my time has been more fully occupied than usual. Tuesday night was Miss Carroll's party; and I wasn't home till—really not early, but late, in the morning. That party very nearly made me late to breakfast. Mr. Davenport was my 'devotedest,' and has called since, which Alice and I think very remarkable. My dear Meg, he's the queerest man! He has the most dejected expression, as if life were the most terrible bore. One would think he had been all through with it before, and didn't enjoy it the first time. He seems to have an exceedingly well-developed taste for grief, and talks in the saddest way about things in general. I think lately his object in life has been to make me think he has some dreadful hidden sorrow. I know he hasn't, by his way; and I talk more nonsense to him in an hour than I ever did to any one else in a day. I cannot help 'taking rises' out of him, as we used to say at school. But he dances well, and knows every thing apparently; and he is ever so much more entertaining to me than the people who are just like every one else. Wednesday he sent me the most exquisite bouquet: it came while Alice and I were out walking. It was raining a little; but we were tired of the house, and went ever so far, having the most delightful talk. You ought to have seen Alice; for the mist gave her more color than usual, and she looked like a beauty, as she is. Oh how I want you to know her, Maggie! I never have said a word hardly about the delightful visit I am having here. Alice's mother, you know, died so long ago that she doesn't remember her at all; and she lived with her aunt till she was old enough for school, and her father travelled and boarded. Now he has taken this delightful house, and she is mistress of it. How she knows the first thing about housekeeping, I cannot imagine! But she certainly succeeds admirably. There never was a girl who had her own way so thoroughly: but her way is always very sensible; and, though she has had the most remarkable chance for becoming a spoiled child, she is the farthest from it. However, I will not expatiate. Thursday night Mr. Thornton gave a whist-party; and—do you think! one of the gentlemen was my Mr. Bruce. I dare say you are making the most awful face, Maggie, but I *will* tell you about him; and why you scold me so I cannot imagine, for I think it is very exciting; and I know there is some good reason for his conduct, for he is a perfect gentleman, every one says; and my only fear is, that I shall never find out about it. I am constantly expecting to hear he is gone: I heard he was to sail last Monday positively. I should feel horridly. When Alice and I found Mr. Thornton had invited him, we laid a bet whether he would accept; but I was right. Mr. Thornton's invitations are seldom refused; but I don't think that was his motive. I won the bet. Yes, he really came, and that wretch of an Alice had the audacity to seat us side by side at supper. He was perfectly polite, but talked very little. I caught him watching me ever and ever so many times; and Alice declares he is in love with me. I wish he would tell me what is the matter with me, for I like him more and more; but don't tell mamma. I have scarcely mentioned him, because I know papa would tell me not to take any notice of him,—and I cannot help it. It is so nice I have you to tell about him. The only queer thing that happened was, in the course of the supper I was saying something to Mr. Dent, who was on my left, about Boston, in answer to some question. Mr. Bruce said, 'Did you ever live in Boston, Miss Tennant?' I answered that our family had always lived there, and I meant to; I had been away at school, however, most of the time for four years. 'Oh!' said he, and began to ask me something else, and stopped suddenly. I wish he had gone on, though perhaps it was only about some Boston people whom he met abroad. He never has been in this country before, you know. And he went on talking with Mr. Bowler, who sat just beyond him, and I found Mr. Dent was talking with Mr. Thornton; so I was left to myself, and was busy for a while over my oysters. I listened to Mr. Bowler and Mr. Bruce, talking about Mr. John Keith's marriage with his mother's nursery-maid, whom he had very sensibly fallen in love with. Mr. Bowler was saying that he had met her, and that she was remarkably ladylike, and did her teacher, whoever she might be, great credit. Mr. Bruce looked up, and saw I was listening,—everybody has been interested in the affair,—and said, 'Oh, yes! I have known several instances of persons, having naturally a great deal of refinement, being taken from a low position when quite grown up, with their tastes and habits apparently firmly established; and, upon their being educated, one could scarcely tell that they had not always been used to the society they were in.' He appealed to me to know if I had not known such cases. I answered that I never had seen any such person myself, but that I had not the least doubt of its being possible. He looked at me a moment, and then said, carelessly as he could, 'Of course you haven't.' And it seemed to me he emphasized the 'you' just the least bit. One might have inferred I was just such a person myself. My dear little sister, what an enormous letter this is. Forgive me if you are bored; and love me dearly, as I do you. Alice sent her love before she went to sleep, where I shall follow her directly. She has been sweetly unconscious of the perplexing Mr. Bruce for at least an hour. I'll tell you every thing else that has happened in my next letter; and do you write very soon to your naughty sister

KITTY

[In the next three or four letters, there is hardly enough mention of Mr. Bruce for me to copy them all out. He seems to be growing more and more agreeable, in spite of his evident determination to the contrary; and as for Miss Kitty, her letters show very plainly what her feelings were toward him; and here is the last of the letters which Miss Margaret Tennant brought, which explains the whole matter, to the great satisfaction of all concerned:—]

Maggy, my cross young sister,

I declare, I'm muddled, as the chambermaid used to say at school. I have fallen into a chronic state of laughter, I'm dying to tell Alice, and have sent for her; but she has callers, and I will begin this very minute to tell you. It is the middle of the morning, but I am just down: I was up very late last night; and oh, we had such fun! Just to think how poor Mr. Bruce and I have puzzled our brains about each other! It is all out now, and I'm so greatly relieved. I never knew how much I cared about it till now. I didn't stop to date my letter, but to-day is Thursday; and Monday morning, as you already know, Aunt Kate came home, to my great delight, though I was broken-hearted to leave Alice's, where I have had such a charming time. Uncle Rob's mother is very much better; and aunty doesn't think she will have to go back, and says I must finish my visit. But I cannot stop to write about that. I came back here in the afternoon; and, Tuesday morning, who should appear but uncle Rob from Savannah, two weeks before we expected him. That night, when he came home to dinner, he said with great glee, 'Kate, I saw young Bruce down town to-day, whom I met in London, and liked so very much. I have invited him to dine with us to-morrow. He is a capital young fellow; and I'm glad we have this young niece to help us entertain him. Have you never met him, Kitty? I'm not going to ask any one else, so I can have him all to myself. I want to ask him about my friends in London; and he tells me he has some letters and messages for me, with which he called at my office, probably just after I went South.' So he rattled on,—you know how fast he talks,—and presently Aunt Kate introduced some other subject, and I wasn't obliged to tell the state of affairs between us. I supposed, of course, Mr. Bruce would treat me in a proper and becoming manner in my uncle's house; and I thought—which proved true—that he might not know I was uncle's niece; and that it might help the matter a little. Oh, it is too funny, Meg! How you will laugh! About dinner-time Mr. Bruce came in with Uncle Rob, and he looked so astonished to see me there; and before uncle Rob had time to get any farther in the introduction than 'Mr. Bruce,' he said, 'Oh, yes! I have met Miss Tennant very often. Is Miss Thornton with you?' Uncle said, 'Kitty, why haven't you told me?' Mr. Bruce looked more surprised when uncle called me 'Kitty;' and, after that, he got more and more involved, as he saw me whisper to aunty, and take some work from a little cabinet, and act as if I belonged here. I explained to Uncle Rob that he had talked so fast the night before, that he didn't give me time to say I knew Mr. Bruce. We didn't wait long for dinner; and the way it was all explained was by my saying, 'Uncle Rob, if you please, I'll have some pepper.' Mr. Bruce started, and really was pale. He looked at me and at Uncle Rob and aunty. I never saw such an expression on any one's face. 'Will you allow me to ask what may seem a very impertinent question?' said he, 'are you Mr. Hunter's niece, Miss Tennant?'—'No,' I answered, 'but I'm Mrs. Hunter's.'—'Oh!' said he, 'I'm inexpressibly relieved: and yet I'm sure it was you; I cannot have been mistaken. There never could be another person so exactly like you, and I remember your face perfectly.' Here he blushed furiously; and, I regret to say, I did too. 'It's a dreadful question to have to ask Mrs. Robert Hunter's niece, and I beg you not to be offended with me; but was it you, or your wraith, who waited upon the table at a house where I dined, just a year ago, in Boston? I haven't the faintest idea what the name was. It was a gentleman to whom I had letters from my father, who had some business with him. He was exceedingly kind to me, and his house was charming; and he had such a pretty little daughter,'—hear that, Meg!—'and I have remembered the table-girl ever since. It cannot have been you; for I have heard you say you were always away at school, except in the summer; and yet I am so sure of your face and figure and hair and every thing about you, only you have lost a strong brogue you had then. Not you, of course, but the person I saw. I have been so foolishly sure about it, and supposed some one had become interested in you, as I was at the time,'—here he blushed again,—'and had educated you where you met Miss Thornton, and that you had a vast deal of tact, and were deluding her and her friends. I have treated you dreadfully, and Miss Alice too; and only the other night I had the most supreme contempt for you, because you were apparently so innocent concerning young women being raised above their station, and all that sort of thing. It would come over me once in a while that you could not be carrying this all out, and I didn't believe in my previous idea at all; and yet the face is the same. I am as much in the dark as ever,' said the poor man solemnly.

"All this time I was pinching my fingers under the table to keep from laughing; but when he stopped, looking to me for a solution of all his troubles, with that ridiculously perplexed face, and I saw uncle Rob's and aunt Kitty's faces, it *would* come, and I fairly shrieked, and rushed from the table into the library, and threw myself into an easy-chair; and I truly never laughed so in my life. I believe I had hysterics at last, and they came in in dismay. *Don't* you know what it was, Margaret? *Don't* you remember the day, last Easter vacation, when Ann had gone down to Salem with her sister, and papa had four strange gentlemen to dine with him, and I put on one of Ann's aprons, and waited on the table for fun? I think it was idiotic in me not to have recognized Mr. Bruce before. Only think how much it would have saved us! He was the handsome young Englishman who went to the drawing-room with you and mamma, instead of the library, and then went away early. You remember all about him now, don't you? I went back to the dining-room, and told the whole story from beginning to end, and if we didn't enjoy ourselves over it! Poor uncle Rob made himself ill with the extent of his laughter, and Mr. Bruce and I are the best of friends. Did you ever know any thing funnier to happen at Mrs. Walkintwo's? If you did, do write me. How I shall enjoy telling papa and mamma! There's Alice coming. Good-by, my dear. But wasn't he a goose?"

"Knowing," said Miss Margaret, "that Kitty has been Mrs. Bruce for nearly thirty years, you can imagine what followed. Mr. Bruce made full amends for his rudeness, and after a while it came to their having long

SARAH ORNE JEWETT

walks and talks together. Uncle Rob approved the match; and, when it was time for her to come home, Mr. Bruce wisely concluded to sail from Boston, and to serve as escort to Aunt Kate and Kitty. So he was all ready to ask papa's consent when he arrived, and it was readily given. He became his father's American partner, and they were married in a year or so, and settled down in the house we left to-night; for Kitty was always loyal to Boston, like the true Tennant that she is. And they have always been the happiest couple in the world, and Kitty's little personification of the absent Ann turned out more happily than her reluctant mamma had any idea of.

"And now," said Miss Margaret, "the storm and the story are both over. It's nearly twelve, and the fire is low. Suppose we go up stairs."

Miss Sydney's Flowers

I

However sensible it may have been considered by other people, it certainly was a disagreeable piece of news to Miss Sydney, that the city authorities had decided to open a new street from St. Mary Street to Jefferson. It seemed a most unwarrantable thing to her that they had a right to buy her property against her will. It was so provoking, that, after so much annoyance from the noise of St. Mary Street during the last dozen years, she must submit to having another public thoroughfare at the side of her house also. If it had only been at the other side, she would not have minded it particularly; for she rarely sat in her drawing-room, which was at the left of the hall. On the right was the library, stately, dismal, and apt to be musty in damp weather; and it would take many bright people, and a blazing wood-fire, and a great deal of sunshine, to make it pleasant. Behind this was the dining-room, which was really bright and sunny, and which opened by wide glass doors into a conservatory. The rattle and clatter of St. Mary Street was not at all troublesome here; and by little and little Miss Sydney had gathered her favorite possessions from other parts of the house, and taken one end of it for her sitting-room. The most comfortable chairs had found their way here, and a luxurious great sofa which had once been in the library, as well as the bookcase which held her favorite books.

The house had been built by Miss Sydney's grandfather, and in his day it had seemed nearly out of the city: now there was only one other house left near it; for one by one the quiet, aristocratic old street had seen its residences give place to shops and warehouses, and Miss Sydney herself had scornfully refused many offers of many thousand dollars for her home. It was so changed! It made her so sad to think of the dear old times, and to see the houses torn down, or the small-paned windows and old-fashioned front-doors replaced with French plate-glass to display better the wares which were to take the places of the quaint furniture and well-known faces of her friends! But Miss Sydney was an old woman, and her friends had diminished sadly. "It seems to me that my invitations are all for funerals in these days," said she to her venerable maid Hannah, who had helped her dress for her parties fifty years before. She had given up society little by little. Her friends had died, or she had allowed herself to drift away from them, while the acquaintances from whom she might have filled their places were only acquaintances still. She was the last of her own family, and, for years before her father died, he had lived mainly in his library, avoiding society and caring for nothing but books; and this, of course, was a check upon his daughter's enjoyment of visitors. Being left to herself, she finally became content with her own society, and since his death, which followed a long illness, she had refused all invitations; and with the exception of the interchange of occasional ceremonious calls with perhaps a dozen families, and her pretty constant attendance at church, you rarely were reminded of her existence. And I must tell the truth: it was not easy to be intimate with her. She was a good woman in a negative kind of way. One never heard of any thing wrong she had done; and if she chose to live alone, and have nothing to do with people, why, it was her own affair. You never seemed to know her any better after a long talk. She had a very fine, courteous way of receiving her guests,—a way of making you feel at your ease more than you imagined you should when with her,—and a stately kind of tact that avoided skilfully much mention of personalities on either side. But mere hospitality is not attractive, for it may be given grudgingly, or, as in her case, from mere habit; for Miss Sydney would never consciously be rude to any one in her own house—or out of it, for that matter. She very rarely came in contact with children; she was not a person likely to be chosen for a confidante by a young girl; she was so cold and reserved, the elder ladies said. She never asked a question about the winter fashions, except of her dressmaker, and she never met with reverses in housekeeping affairs, and these two facts rendered her unsympathetic to many. She was fond of reading, and enjoyed heartily the pleasant people she met in books. She appreciated their good qualities, their thoughtfulness, kindness, wit, or sentiment; but the thought never suggested itself to her mind that there were living people not far away, who could give her all this, and more.

If calling were not a regulation of society, if one only went to see the persons one really cared for, I am afraid Miss Sydney would soon have been quite forgotten. Her character would puzzle many people. She put no visible hinderance in your way; for I do not think she was consciously reserved and cold. She was thoroughly well-bred, rich, and in her way charitable; that is, she gave liberally to public subscriptions which came under her notice, and to church contributions. But she got on, somehow, without having friends; and, though the loss of one had always been a real grief, she learned without much trouble the way of living the lonely, comfortable, but very selfish life, and the way of being the woman I have tried to describe. There were occasional days when she was tired of herself, and life seemed an empty, formal, heartless discipline. Her wisest acquaintances pitied her loneliness; and busy, unselfish people wondered how she could be deaf to the teachings of her good clergyman, and blind to all the chances of usefulness and happiness which the world afforded her; and others still envied her, and wondered to whom she meant to leave all her money.

I began by telling you of the new street. It was suggested that it should bear the name of Sydney; but the authorities decided finally to compliment the country's chief magistrate, and call it Grant Place. Miss Sydney did not like the sound of it. Her family had always been indifferent to politics, and indeed the kite of the Sydneys had flown for many years high above the winds that affect commonplace people. The new way from Jefferson Street to St. Mary was a great convenience, and it seemed to our friend that all the noisiest vehicles in the city had a preference for going back and forth under her windows. You see she did not suspect, what afterward became so evident, that there was to be a way opened into her own heart also, and that she should confess one day, long after, that she might have died a selfish old woman, and not have left one sorry face behind her, if it had not been for the cutting of Grant Place.

The side of her conservatory was now close upon the sidewalk, and this certainly was not agreeable. She could not think of putting on her big gardening-apron, and going in to work among her dear plants any more, with all the world staring in at her as it went by. John the coachman, who had charge of the greenhouse, was at first very indignant; but, after he found that his flowers were noticed and admired, his anger was turned into an ardent desire to merit admiration, and he kept his finest plants next the street. It was a good thing for the greenhouse, because it had never been so carefully tended; and plant after plant was forced into luxuriant foliage and blossom. He and Miss Sydney had planned at first to have close wire screens made to match those in the dining-room; but now, when she spoke of his hurrying the workmen, whom she supposed had long since been ordered to make them, John said, "Indeed, mum, it would be the ruin of the plants shutting out the light; and they would all be rusted with the showerings I gives them every day." And Miss Sydney smiled, and said no more.

The street was opened late in October, and, soon after, cold weather began in real earnest. Down in that business part of the city it was the strangest, sweetest surprise to come suddenly upon the long line of blooming plants and tall green lily-leaves under a roof festooned with roses and trailing vines. For the first two or three weeks, almost everybody stopped, if only for a moment. Few of Miss Sydney's own friends even had ever seen her greenhouse; for they were almost invariably received in the drawing-room. Gentlemen stopped the thought of business affairs, and went on down the street with a fresher, happier feeling. And the tired shop-girls lingered longest. Many a man and woman thought of some sick person to whom a little handful of the green leaves and bright blossoms, with their coolness and freshness, would bring so much happiness. And it was found, long months afterward, that a young man had been turned back from a plan of wicked mischief by the sight of a tall, green geranium, like one that bloomed in his mother's sitting-room way up in the country. He had not thought, for a long time before, of the dear old woman who supposed her son was turning his wits to good account in the city. But Miss Sydney did not know how much he wished for a bit to put in his buttonhole when she indignantly went back to the dining-room to wait until that impertinent fellow stopped staring in.

II

IT WAS JUST ABOUT THIS time that Mrs. Marley made a change in her place of business. She had sold candy round the corner in Jefferson Street for a great many years; but she had suffered terribly from rheumatism all the winter before. She was nicely sheltered from too much sun in the summer; but the north winds of winter blew straight toward her; and after much deliberation, and many fears and questionings as to the propriety of such an act, she had decided to find another stand. You or I would think at first that it could make no possible difference where she sat in the street with her goods; but in fact one has regular customers in that business, as well as in the largest wholesale enterprise. There was some uncertainty whether these friends would follow her if she went away. Mrs. Marley's specialty was molasses-candy; and I am sure, if you ever chanced to eat any of it, you would look out for the old lady next time you went along the street. Times seemed very hard this winter. Not that trade had seriously diminished; but still the outlook was very dark. Mrs. Marley was old, and had been so for some years, so she was used to that; but somehow this fall she seemed to be growing very much older all of a sudden. She found herself very tired at night, and she was apt to lose her breath if she moved quickly; besides this, the rheumatism tortured her. She had saved only a few dollars, though she and her sister had had a comfortable living,—what they had considered comfortable, at least, though they sometimes had been hungry, and very often cold. They would surely go to the almshouse sooner or later,—she and her lame old sister Polly.

It was Polly who made the candy which Mrs. Marley sold. Their two little rooms were up three flights of stairs; and Polly, being too lame to go down herself, had not been out of doors in seven years. There was nothing but roofs and sky to be seen from the windows; and, as there was a manufactory near, the sky was apt to be darkened by its smoke. Some of the neighbors dried their clothes on the roofs, and Polly used to be very familiar with the apparel of the old residents, and exceedingly interested when a strange family came, and she saw something new. There was a little bright pink dress that the trig young French woman opposite used to hang out to dry; and somehow poor old Polly used always to be brightened and cheered by the sight of it. Once in a while she caught a glimpse of the child who wore it. She hardly ever thought now of the outside world when left to herself, and on the whole she was not discontented. Sister Becky used to have a great deal to tell her sometimes of an evening. When Mrs. Marley told her in the spring twilight that the grass in the square was growing green, and that she had heard a robin, it used to make Polly feel homesick; for she was apt to think much of her childhood, and she had been born in the country. She was very deaf, poor soul, and her world was a very forlorn one. It was nearly always quite silent, it was very small and smoky out of doors, and very dark and dismal within. Sometimes it was a hopeless world, because the candy burnt; and if there had not been her Bible and hymn-book, and a lame pigeon that lit on the window-sill to be fed every morning, Miss Polly would have found her time go heavily.

One night Mrs. Marley came into the room with a cheerful face, and said very loud, "Polly, I've got some news!" Polly knew by her speaking so loud that she was in good-humor. When any thing discouraging had happened, Becky spoke low, and then was likely to be irritated when asked to repeat her remark.

"Dear heart!" said Mrs. Marley, "now I am glad you had something hot for supper. I was turning over in my mind what we could cook up, for I feel real hollow. It's a kind of chilly day." And she sat down by the stove, while Polly hobbled to the table, with one hand to her ear to catch the first sound of the good news, and the other holding some baked potatoes in her apron. That hand was twisted with rheumatism, for the disease ran in the family. She was afraid every day that she should have to give up making the candy on the next; for it hurt her so to use it. She was continually being harrowed by the idea of its becoming quite useless, and that the candy might not be so good; and then what would become of them? Becky Marley was often troubled by the same thought. Yet they were almost always good-natured, poor old women; and, though Polly Sharpe's pleasures and privileges were by far the fewest of anybody's I ever knew, I think she was as glad in those days to know the dandelions were in bloom as if she could see them; and she got more good from the fragments of the Sunday-morning sermon that sister Becky brought home than many a listener did from the whole service.

The potatoes were done to a turn, Mrs. Marley shouted; and then Polly sat down close by her to hear the news.

"You know I have been worrying about the cold weather a-coming, and my rheumatics; and I was afeared to change my stand, on account of losing custom. Well, to-day it all come over me to once that I might move down a piece on Grant Place,—that new street that's cut through to St. Mary. I've noticed for some time past that almost all my reg'lar customers turns down that way, so this morning I thought I'd step down that way too, and see if there was a chance. And after I gets into the street I sees people stopping and looking at something as they went along; and so I goes down to see; and it is one of them hothouses, full of plants a-growing like it was mid-summer. It belongs to the big Sydney house on the corner. There's a good place to sit right at the corner of it, and I'm going to move over there to-morrow. I thought as how I wouldn't leave Jefferson Street to-day, for it was too sudden. You see folks stops and looks at the plants, and there wasn't any wind there to-day. There! I wish you could see them flowers."

Sister Polly was very pleased, and, after the potatoes and bread were eaten, she brought on an apple pie that had been sent up by Mrs. Welch, the washer-woman who lived on the floor next but one below. She was going away for three or four days, having been offered good pay to do some cleaning in a new house, and her board besides, near her work. So you see that evening was quite a jubilee.

The next day Mrs. Marley's wildest expectations were realized; for she was warm as toast the whole morning, and sold all her candy, and went home by two o'clock. That had never happened but once or twice before. "Why, I shouldn't wonder if we could lay up considerable this winter," said she to Polly.

Miss Sydney did not like the idea of the old candy-woman's being there. Children came to buy of her, and the street seemed noisier than ever at times. Perhaps she might have to leave the house, after all. But one may get used to almost any thing; and as the days went by she was surprised to find that she was not half so much annoyed as at first; and one afternoon she found herself standing at one of the dining-room windows, and watching the people go by. I do not think she had shown so much interest as this in the world at large for many years. I think it must have been from noticing the pleasure her flowers gave the people who stopped to look at them that she began to think herself selfish, and to be aware how completely indifferent she had grown to any claims the world might have upon her. And one morning, when she heard somebody say, "Why, it's like a glimpse into the tropics! Oh! I wish I could have such a conservatory!" she thought, "Here I have kept this all to myself for all these years, when so many others might have enjoyed it too!" But then the old feeling of independence came over her. The greenhouse was out of people's way; she surely couldn't have let people in whom she didn't know; however, she was glad, now that the street was cut, that some one had more pleasure, if she had not. After all, it was a satisfaction to our friend; and from this time the seeds of kindness and charity and helpfulness began to show themselves above the ground in the almost empty garden of her heart. I will tell you how they grew and blossomed; and as strangers came to see her real flowers, and to look in at the conservatory windows from the cold city street, instead of winter to see a bit of imprisoned summer, so friend after friend came to find there was another garden in her own heart, and Miss Sydney learned the blessedness there is in loving and giving and helping.

For it is sure we never shall know what it is to lack friends, if we keep our hearts ready to receive them. If we are growing good and kind and helpful, those who wish for help and kindness will surely find us out. A tree covered with good fruit is never unnoticed in the fields. If

SARAH ORNE JEWETT

we bear thorns and briers, we can't expect people to take very great pains to come and gather them. It is thought by many persons to be not only a bad plan, but an ill-bred thing, to give out to more than a few carefully selected friends. But it came to her more and more that there was great selfishness and short-sightedness in this. One naturally has a horror of dragging the secrets and treasures of one's heart and thought out to the light of day. One may be willing to go without the good that may come to one's own self through many friendships; but, after all, God does not teach us, and train our lives, only that we may come to something ourselves. He helps men most through other men's lives; and we must take from him, and give out again, all we can, wherever we can, remembering that the great God is always trying to be the friend of the least of us. The danger is, that we oftenest give our friendship selfishly; we do not think of our friends, but of ourselves. One never can find one's self beggared; love is a treasure that does not lessen, but grows, as we spend it.

The passers-by seemed so delighted with some new plants which she and John had arranged one day, that, as she was going out in the afternoon to drive, she stopped just as she was going to step into the carriage, and said she thought she would go round and look at the conservatory from the outside. So John turned the horses, and followed. It was a very cold day, and there were few people in the street. Every thing was so cheerless out of doors, and the flowers looked so summer-like! No wonder the people liked to stop, poor souls! For the richer, more comfortable ones lived farther up town. It was not in the shopping region; and, except the business-men who went by morning and evening, almost every one was poor.

Miss Sydney had never known what the candy-woman sold before, for she could not see any thing but the top of her rusty black bonnet from the window. But now she saw that the candy was exactly like that she and her sister used to buy years upon years ago; and she stopped to speak to the old woman, and to buy some, to the utter amazement of her coachman. Mrs. Marley was excited by so grand a customer, and was a great while counting out the drumsticks, and wrapping them up. While Miss Sydney stood there, a thin, pitiful little girl came along, carrying a clumsy baby. They stopped, and the baby tried to reach down for a piece. The girl was quite as wistful; but she pulled him back, and walked on to the flowers. "Oh! pitty, pitty!" said the baby, while the dirty little hands patted the glass delightedly.

"Move along there," said John gruffly; for it was his business to keep that glass clean and bright.

The girl looked round, frightened, and, seeing that the coachman was big and cross-looking, the forlorn little soul went away. "Baby want to walk? You're so heavy!" said she in a fretful, tired way. But the baby was half crying, and held her tight. He had meant to stay some time longer, and look at those pretty, bright things, since he could not have the candy.

Mrs. Marley felt as if her customer might think her stingy, and proceeded to explain that she couldn't think of giving her candy away. "Bless you, ma'am, I wouldn't have a stick left by nine o'clock."

Miss Sydney "never gave money to street-beggars." But these children had not begged, and somehow she pitied them very much, they looked so hungry. And she called them back. There was a queer tone to her voice; and she nearly cried after she had given the package of candy to them, and thrown a dollar upon the board in front of Mrs. Marley, and found herself in the carriage, driving away. Had she been very silly? and what could John have thought? But the children were so glad; and the old candy-woman had said, "God bless you, mum!"

After this, Miss Sydney could not keep up her old interest in her own affairs. She felt restless and dissatisfied, and wondered how she could have done the same things over and over so contentedly for so many years. You may be sure, that, if Grant Place had been unthought of, she would have lived on in the same fashion to the end of her days. But after this she used to look out of the window; and she sat a great deal in the conservatory, when it was not too warm there, behind some tall callas. The servants found her usually standing in the dining-room; for she listened for footsteps, and was half-ashamed to have them notice that she had changed in the least. We are all given to foolish behavior of this kind once in a while. We are often restrained because we feel bound to conform to people's idea of us. We must be such persons as we imagine our friends think us to be. They believe that we have made up our minds about them, and are apt to show us only that behavior which they think we expect. They are afraid of us sometimes. They think we cannot sympathize with them. Our friend felt almost as if she were yielding to some sin in this strange interest in the passers-by. She had lived so monotonous a life, that any change could not have failed to be somewhat alarming. She told Bessie Thorne afterward, that one day she came upon that verse of Keble's Hymn for St. Matthew's Day. Do you remember it?—

"There are, in this loud, stunning tide
Of human care and crime,
With whom the melodies abide
Of the everlasting chime;
Who carry music in their heart
Through dusky lane and wrangling mart,
Plying their daily task with busier feet
Because their secret souls a holy strain repeat."

It seemed as if it were a message to herself, and she could not help going to the window a few minutes afterward. The faces were mostly tired-looking and dissatisfied. Some people looked very eager and hurried, but none very contented. It was the literal daily bread they thought of; and, when two fashionably-dressed ladies chanced to go by the window, their faces were strangely like their poorer neighbors in expression. Miss Sydney wondered what the love for one's neighbor could be; if she could ever feel it herself. She did not even like these people whom she watched, and yet every day, for years and years, she had acknowledged them her brothers and sisters when she said, "Our Father who art in heaven."

It seemed as if Miss Sydney, of all people, might have been independent and unfettered. It is so much harder for us who belong to a family for we are hindered by the thought of people's noticing our attempts at reform. It is like surrendering some opinion ignominiously which we have fought for. It is a kind of "giving in." But when she had acknowledged to herself that she had been in the wrong, that she was a selfish, thoughtless old woman, that she was alone, without friends, and it had been her own fault, she was puzzled to know how to do better. She could not begin to be very charitable all at once. The more she realized what her own character had become, the more hopeless and necessary seemed reform.

Such times as this come to many of us, both in knowing ourselves and our friends. An awakening, one might call it,—an opening of the blind eyes of our spiritual selves. And our ears are open to some of the voices which call us; while others might as well be silent, for all the heed we give them. We go on, from day to day, doing, with more or less faithfulness, that part of our work we have wit enough to comprehend; but one day suddenly we are shown a broader field, stretching out into the distance, and know that from this also we may bring in a harvest by and by, and with God's help.

Miss Sydney meant to be better,—not alone for the sake of having friends, not alone to quiet her conscience, but because she knew she had been so far from living a Christian life, and she was bitterly ashamed. This was all she needed,—all any of us need,—to know that we must be better men and women for God's sake; that we cannot be better without his help, and that his help may be had for the asking. But where should she begin? She had always treated her servants kindly, and they were the people she knew best. She would surely try to be more interested in the friends she met; but it was nearly Christmas time, and people rarely came to call. Every one was busy. Becky Marley's cheery face haunted her; and one day after having looked down from the window on the top of her bonnet, she remembered that she did not get any candy, after all, and she would go round to see the old lady again, she looked poor, and she would give her some money. Miss Sydney dressed herself for the street, and closed the door behind her very carefully, as if she were a mischievous child running away. It was very cold, and there were hardly a dozen persons to be seen in the streets, and Mrs. Marley had evidently been crying.

"I should like some of your candy," said our friend. "You know I didn't take any, after all, the other day." And then she felt very conscious and awkward, fearing that the candy-woman thought she wished to remind her of her generosity.

"Two of the large packages, if you please. But, dear me! aren't you very cold, sitting here in the wind?" and Miss Sydney shivered, in spite of her warm wrappings.

It was the look of sympathy that was answered first, for it was more comforting than even the prospect of money, sorely as Mrs. Marley needed that.

"Yes, mum, I've had the rheumatics this winter awful. But the wind here!—why, it ain't nothing to what it blows round in Jefferson Street, where I used to sit. I shouldn't be out to-day, but I was called upon sudden to pay my molasses bill, when I'd just paid my rent; and I don't know how ever I can. There's sister Polly—she's dead lame and deaf. I s'pose we'll both be in the almshouse afore spring. I'm an old woman to be earning a living out o' doors in winter weather."

There was no mistaking the fact that Miss Sydney was in earnest when she said, "I'm so sorry! Can't I help you?"

Somehow she did not feel so awkward, and she enjoyed very much hearing this bit of confidence.

"But my trade has improved wonderful since I came here. People mostly stops to see them beautiful flowers; and then they sees me, and stops and buys something. Well, there's some days when I gets down-hearted, and I just looks up there, and sees them flowers blooming so cheerful, and I says, 'There! this world ain't all cold and poor and old, like I be; and the Lord he ain't never tired of us, with our worrying about what he's a-doing with us; and heaven's a-coming before long anyhow!'" And the Widow Marley stopped to dry her eyes with the corner of her shawl.

Miss Sydney asked her to go round to the kitchen, and warm herself; and, on finding out more of her new acquaintance's difficulties, she sent her home happy, with money enough to pay the dreaded bill, and a basket of good things which furnished such a supper for herself and sister Polly as they had not seen for a long time. And their fortunes were bettered from that day. "If it hadn't been for the flowers, I should ha' been freezing my old bones on Jefferson Street this minute, I s'pose," said the Widow Marley.

Miss Sydney went back to the dining-room after her *protégée* had gone, and felt a comfortable sense of satisfaction in what she had done. It had all come about in such an easy way too! A little later she went into the conservatory, and worked among her plants. She really felt so much younger and happier; and once, as she stood still, looking at some lilies-of-the-valley that John had been forcing into bloom, she did not notice that a young lady was looking through the window at her very earnestly.

III

That same evening Mrs. Thorne and Bessie were sitting up late in their library. It was snowing very fast, and had been since three o'clock; and no one had called. They had begun the evening by reading and writing, and now were ending it with a talk.

"Mamma," said Bessie, after there had been a pause, "whom do you suppose I have taken a fancy to? And do you know, I pity her so much!—Miss Sydney."

"But I don't know that she is so much to be pitied," said Mrs. Thorne, smiling at the enthusiastic tone. "She must have every thing she wants. She lives all alone, and hasn't any intimate friends, but, if a person chooses such a life, why, what can we do? What made you think of her?"

"I have been trying to think of one real friend she has. Everybody is polite enough to her, and I never heard that any one disliked her; but she must be forlorn sometimes. I came through that new street by her house to-day: that's how I happened to think of her. Her greenhouse is perfectly beautiful, and I stopped to look in. I always supposed she was cold as ice (I'm sure she looks so); but she was standing out in one corner, looking down at some flowers with just the sweetest face. Perhaps she is shy. She used to be very good-natured to me when I was a child, and used to go there with you. I don't think she knows me since I came home: at any rate, I mean to go to see her some day."

"I certainly would," said Mrs. Thorne. "She will be perfectly polite to you, at all events. And perhaps she may be lonely, though I rather doubt it; not that I wish to discourage you, my dear. I haven't seen her in a long time, for we have missed each other's calls. She never went into society much; but she used to be a very elegant woman, and is now, for that matter."

"I pity her," said Bessie persistently. "I think I should be very fond of her if she would let me. She looked so kind as she stood among the flowers to-day! I wonder what she was thinking about. Oh! do you think she would mind if I asked her to give me some flowers for the hospital?"

Bessie Thorne is a very dear girl. Miss Sydney must have been hard-hearted if she had received her coldly one afternoon a few days afterward, she seemed so refreshingly young and girlish a guest as she rose to meet the mistress of that solemn, old-fashioned drawing-room. Miss Sydney had had a re-action from the pleasure her charity had given her, and was feeling bewildered, unhappy, and old that day. "What can she wish to see me for, I wonder?" thought she, as she closed her book, and looked at Miss Thorne's card herself, to be sure the servant had read it right. But, when she saw the girl herself, her pleasure showed itself unmistakably in her face.

"Are you really glad to see me?" said Bessie in her frankest way, with a very gratified smile. "I was afraid you might think it was very odd in me to come. I used to like so much to call upon you with mamma when I was a little girl! And the other day I saw you in your conservatory, and I have wished to come and see you ever since."

"I am very glad to see you, my dear," said Miss Sydney, for the second time. "I have been quite forgotten by the young people of late years. I was sorry to miss Mrs. Thorne's call. Is she quite well? I meant to return it one day this week, and I thought only last night I would ask about you. You have been abroad, I think?"

Was not this an auspicious beginning? I cannot tell you all that happened that afternoon, for I have told so long a story already. But you will imagine it was the beginning of an intimacy that gave great pleasure, and did great good, to both the elder woman and the younger. It is hard to tell the pleasure which the love and friendship of a fresh, bright girl like Bessie Thorne, may give an older person. There is such a satisfaction in being convinced that one is still interesting and still lovable, though the years that are gone have each kept some gift or grace, and the possibilities of life seem to have been realized and decided. There are days of our old age when there seems so little left in life, that living is a mere formality. This busy world seems done with the old, however dear their memories of it, however strong their claims upon it. They are old: their life now is only waiting and resting. It may be quite right that we sometimes speak of second childhood, because we must be children before we are grown; and the life to come must find us, will find us, ready for service. Our old people have lived in the world so long; they think they know it so well: but the young man is master of the trade of living, and the old man only his blundering apprentice.

Miss Sydney's solemnest and most unprepared servant was startled to find Bessie Thorne and his mistress sitting cosily together before the dining-room fire. Bessie had a paper full of cut flowers to leave at the Children's Hospital on her way home. Miss Sydney had given liberally to the contribution for that object; but she never had suspected how interesting it was until Bessie told her, and she said she should like to go some day, and see the building and its occupants for herself. And the girl told her of other interests that were near her kind young heart,— not all charitable interests,—and they parted intimate friends.

"I never felt such a charming certainty of being agreeable," wrote Bessie that night to a friend of hers. "She seemed so interested in every thing, and, as I told you, so pleased with my coming to see her. I have promised to go there very often. She told me in the saddest way that she had been feeling so old and useless and friendless, and she was very confidential. Imagine her being confidential with me! She seemed to me just like myself as I was last year,—you remember,—just beginning to realize what life ought to be, and trying, in a frightened, blind kind of way, to be good and useful. She said she was just beginning to understand her selfishness. She told me I had done her ever so much good; and I couldn't help the tears coming into my eyes. I wished so much you were there, or some one who could help her more; but I suppose God knew when he sent me. Doesn't it seem strange that an old woman should talk to me in this way, and come to me for help? I am afraid people would laugh at the very idea. And only to think of her living on and on, year after year, and then being changed so! She kissed me when I came away, and I carried the flowers to the hospital. I shall always be fond of that conservatory, because, if I hadn't stopped to look in that day, I might never have thought of her.

"There was one strange thing happened, which I must tell you about, though it is so late. She has grown very much interested in an old candy-woman, and told me about her; and do you know that this evening uncle Jack came in, and asked if we knew of anybody who would do for janitress—at the Natural History rooms, I think he said. There is good pay, and she would just sell catalogues, and look after things a little. Of course the candy-woman may not be competent; but, from what Miss Sydney told me, I think she is just the person."

The next Sunday the minister read this extract from "Queen's Gardens" in his sermon. Two of his listeners never had half understood its meaning before as they did then. Bessie was in church, and Miss Sydney suddenly turned her head, and smiled at her young friend, to the great amazement of the people who sat in the pews near by. What *could* have come over Miss Sydney?

"The path of a good woman is strewn with flowers; but they rise *behind* her steps, not before them. 'Her feet have touched the meadow, and left the daisies rosy.' Flowers flourish in the garden of one who loves them. A pleasant magic it would be if you could flush flowers into brighter bloom by a kind look upon them; nay, more, if a look had the power not only to cheer but to guard them. This you would think a great thing? And do you think it not a greater thing that all this, and more than this, you can do for fairer flowers than these,—flowers that could bless you for having blessed them, and will love you for having loved them,—flowers that have eyes like yours, and thoughts like yours, and lives like yours?"

SARAH ORNE JEWETT

LADY FERRY

We have an instinctive fear of death; yet we have a horror of a life prolonged far beyond the average limit: it is sorrowful; it is pitiful; it has no attractions.

This world is only a schoolroom for the larger life of the next. Some leave it early, and some late: some linger long after they seem to have learned all its lessons. This world is no heaven: its pleasures do not last even through our little lifetimes.

There are many fables of endless life, which in all ages have caught the attention of men; we are familiar with the stories of the old patriarchs who lived their hundreds of years: but one thinks of them wearily, and without envy.

WHEN I WAS A CHILD, it was necessary that my father and mother should take a long sea-voyage. I never had been separated from them before; but at this time they thought it best to leave me behind, as I was not strong, and the life on board ship did not suit me. When I was told of this decision, I was very sorry, and at once thought I should be miserable without my mother; besides, I pitied myself exceedingly for losing the sights I had hoped to see in the country which they were to visit. I had an uncontrollable dislike to being sent to school, having in some way been frightened by a maid of my mother's, who had put many ideas and aversions into my head which I was many years in outgrowing. Having dreaded this possibility, it was a great relief to know that I was not to be sent to school at all, but to be put under the charge of two elderly cousins of my father,—a gentleman and his wife whom I had once seen, and liked dearly. I knew that their home was at a fine old-fashioned country-place, far from town, and close beside a river, and I was pleased with this prospect, and at once began to make charming plans for the new life.

I had lived always with grown people, and seldom had had any thing to do with children. I was very small for my age, and a strange mixture of childishness and maturity; and, having the appearance of being absorbed in my own affairs, no one ever noticed me much, or seemed to think it better that I should not listen to the conversation. In spite of considerable curiosity, I followed an instinct which directed me never to ask questions at these times: so I often heard stray sentences which puzzled me, and which really would have been made simple and commonplace at once, if I had only asked their meaning. I was, for the most of the time, in a world of my own. I had a great deal of imagination, and was always telling myself stories; and my mind was adrift in these so much, that my real absent-mindedness was mistaken for childish unconcern. Yet I was a thoroughly simple, unaffected child. My dreams and thoughtfulness gave me a certain tact and perception unusual in a child; but my pleasures were as deep in simple things as heart could wish.

It happened that our cousin Matthew was to come to the city on business the week that the ship was to sail, and that I could stay with my father and mother to the very last day, and then go home with him. This was much pleasanter than leaving sooner under the care of an utter stranger, as was at first planned. My cousin Agnes wrote a kind letter about my coming which seemed to give her much pleasure. She remembered me very well, and sent me a message which made me feel of consequence; and I was delighted with the plan of making her so long a visit.

One evening I was reading a story-book, and I heard my father say in an undertone, "How long has madam been at the ferry this last time? Eight or ten years, has she not? I suppose she is there yet?"—"Oh, yes!" said my mother, "or Agnes would have told us. She spoke of her in the last letter you had, while we were in Sweden."

"I should think she would be glad to have a home at last, after her years of wandering about. Not that I should be surprised now to hear that she had disappeared again. When I was staying there while I was young, we thought she had drowned herself, and even had the men search for her along the shore of the river; but after a time cousin Matthew heard of her alive and well in Salem; and I believe she appeared again this last time as suddenly as she went away."

"I suppose she will never die," said my mother gravely. "She must be terribly old," said my father. "When I saw her last, she had scarcely changed at all from the way she looked when I was a boy. She is even more quiet and gentle than she used to be. There is no danger that the child will have any fear of her; do you think so?"—"Oh, no! but I think I will tell her that madam is a very old woman, and that I hope she will be very kind, and try not to annoy her; and that she must not be frightened at her strange notions. I doubt if she knows what craziness is."—"She would be wise if she could define it," said my father with a smile. "Perhaps we had better say nothing about the old lady. It is probable that she stays altogether in her own room, and that the child will rarely see her. I never have realized until lately the horror of such a long life as hers, living on and on, with one's friends gone long ago: such an endless life in this world!"

Then there was a mysterious old person living at the ferry, and there was a question whether I would not be "afraid" of her. She "had not changed" since my father was a boy: "it was horrible to have one's life endless in this world!"

The days went quickly by. My mother, who was somewhat of an invalid, grew sad as the time drew near for saying good-by to me, and was more tender and kind than ever before, and more indulgent of every wish and fancy of mine. We had been together all my life, and now it was to be long months before she could possibly see my face again, and perhaps she was leaving me forever. Her time was all spent, I believe, in thoughts for me, and in making arrangements for my comfort. I did see my mother again; but the tears fill my eyes when I think how dear we became to each other before that first parting, and with what a lingering, loving touch, she herself packed my boxes, and made sure, over and over again, that I had whatever I should need; and I remember how close she used to hold me when I sat in her lap in the evening, saying that she was afraid I should have grown too large to be held when she came back again. We had more to say to each other than ever before, and I think, until then, that my mother never had suspected how much I observed of life and of older people in a certain way; that I was something more than a little child who went from one interest to another carelessly. I have known since that my mother's childhood was much like mine. She, however, was timid, while I had inherited from my father his fearlessness, and lack of suspicion; and these qualities, like a fresh wind, swept away any cobwebs of nervous anticipation and sensitiveness. Every one was kind to me, partly, I think because I interfered with no one. I was glad of the kindness, and, with my unsuspected dreaming and my happy childishness, I had gone through life with almost perfect contentment, until this pain of my first real loneliness came into my heart.

It was a day's journey to cousin Matthew's house, mostly by rail; though, toward the end, we had to travel a considerable distance by stage, and at last were left on the river-bank opposite my new home, and I saw a boat waiting to take us across. It was just at sunset, and

I remember wondering if my father and mother were out of sight of land, and if they were watching the sky; if my father would remember that only the evening before we had gone out for a walk together, and there had been a sunset so much like this. It somehow seemed long ago. Cousin Matthew was busy talking with the ferryman; and indeed he had found acquaintances at almost every part of the journey, and had not been much with me, though he was kind and attentive in his courteous, old-fashioned way, treating me with the same ceremonious politeness which he had shown my mother. He pointed out the house to me: it was but a little way from the edge of the river. It was very large and irregular, with great white chimneys; and, while the river was all in shadow, the upper windows of two high gables were catching the last red glow of the sun. On the opposite side of a green from the house were the farm-house and buildings; and the green sloped down to the water, where there was a wharf and an ancient-looking storehouse. There were some old boats and long sticks of timber lying on the shore; and I saw a flock of white geese march solemnly up toward the barns. From the open green I could see that a road went up the hill beyond. The trees in the garden and orchard were the richest green; their round tops were clustered thick together; and there were some royal great elms near the house. The fiery red faded from the high windows as we came near the shore, and cousin Agnes was ready to meet me; and when she put her arms round me as kindly as my mother would have done, and kissed me twice in my father's fashion, was sure that I loved her, and would be contented. Her hair was very gray; but she did not look, after all, so very old. Her face was a grave one, as if she had had many cares; yet they had all made her stronger, and there had been some sweetness, and something to be glad about, and to thank God for, in every sorrow. I had a feeling always that she was my sure defence and guard. I was safe and comfortable with her: it was the same feeling which one learns to have toward God more and more, as one grows older.

We went in through a wide hall, and up stairs, through a long passage, to my room, which was in a corner of one of the gables. Two windows looked on the garden and the river: another looked across to the other gable, and into the square, grassy court between. It was a rambling, great house, and seemed like some English houses I had seen. It would be great fun to go into all the rooms some day soon.

"How much you are like your father!" said cousin Agnes, stooping to kiss me again, with her hand on my shoulder. I had a sudden consciousness of my bravery in having behaved so well all day; then I remembered that my father and mother were at every instant being carried farther and farther away. I could almost hear the waves dash about the ship; and I could not help crying a little. "Poor little girl!" said cousin Agnes: "I am very sorry." And she sat down, and took me in her lap for a few minutes. She was tall, and held me so comfortably, and I soon was almost happy again; for she hoped I would not be lonely with her, and that I would not think she was a stranger, for she had known and loved my father so well; and it would make cousin Matthew so disappointed and uneasy if I were discontented; and would I like some bread and milk with my supper, in the same blue china bowl, with the dragon on it, which my father used to have when he was a boy? These arguments were by no means lost upon me, and I was ready to smile presently; and then we went down to the dining-room, which had some solemn-looking portraits on the walls, and heavy, stiff furniture; and there was an old-fashioned woman standing ready to wait, whom cousin Agnes called Deborah, and who smiled at me graciously.

Cousin Matthew talked with his wife for a time about what had happened to him and to her during his absence; and then he said, "And how is madam to-day? you have not spoken of her."—"She is not so well as usual," said cousin Agnes. "She has had one of her sorrowful times since you went away. I have sat with her for several hours to-day; but she has hardly spoken to me." And then cousin Matthew looked at me, and cousin Agnes hesitated for a minute. Deborah had left the room.

"We speak of a member of our family whom you have not seen, although you may have heard your father speak of her. She is called Lady Ferry by most people who know of her; but you may say madam when you speak to her. She is very old, and her mind wanders, so that she has many strange fancies; but you must not be afraid, for she is very gentle and harmless. She is not used to children; but I know you will not annoy her, and I dare say you can give her much pleasure." This was all that was said; but I wished to know more. It seemed to me that there was a reserve about this person, and the old house itself was the very place for a mystery. As I went through some of the other rooms with cousin Agnes in the summer twilight, I half expected to meet Lady Ferry in every shadowy corner; but I did not dare to ask a question. My father's words came to me,—"Such an endless life," and "living on and on." And why had he and my mother never spoken to me afterward of my seeing her? They had talked about it again, perhaps, and did not mean to tell me, after all.

I saw something of the house that night, the great kitchen, with its huge fireplace, and other rooms up stairs and down; and cousin Agnes told me, that by daylight I should go everywhere, except to Madam's rooms: I must wait for an invitation there.

The house had been built a hundred and fifty years before, by Colonel Haverford, an Englishman, whom no one knew much about, except that he lived like a prince, and would never tell his history. He and his sons died; and after the Revolution the house was used for a tavern for many years,—the Ferry Tavern,—and the place was busy enough. Then there was a bridge built down the river, and the old ferry fell into disuse; and the owner of the house died, and his family also died, or went away; and then the old place, for a long time, was either vacant, or in the hands of different owners. It was going to ruin at length, when cousin Matthew bought it, and came there from the city to live years before. He was a strange man; indeed, I know now that all the possessors of the Ferry farm must have been strange men. One often hears of the influence of climate upon character; there is a strong influence of place; and the inanimate things which surround us indoors and out make us follow out in our lives their own silent characteristics. We unconsciously catch the tone of every house in which we live, and of every view of the outward, material world which grows familiar to us, and we are influenced by surroundings nearer and closer still than the climate or the country which we inhabit. At the old Haverford house it was mystery which one felt when one entered the door; and when one came away, after cordiality, and days of sunshine and pleasant hospitality, it was still with a sense of this mystery, and of something unseen and unexplained. Not that there was any thing covered and hidden necessarily; but it was the quiet undertone in the house which had grown to be so old, and had known the magnificent living of Colonel Haverford's time, and afterward the struggles of poor gentlemen and women, who had hardly warmed its walls with their pitiful fires, and shivering, hungry lives; then the long procession of travellers who had been sheltered there in its old tavern days; finally, my cousin Matthew and his wife, who had made it their home, when, with all their fortune, they felt empty-handed, and as if their lives were ended, because their only son had died. Here they had learned to be happy again in a quiet sort of way, and had become older and serener, loving this lovable place by the river, and keepers of its secret—whatever that might be.

I was wide awake that first evening: I was afraid of being sent to bed, and, to show cousin Agnes that I was not sleepy, I chattered far more than usual. It was warm, and the windows of the parlor where we sat looked upon the garden. The moon had risen, and it was light out of doors. I caught every now and then the faint smell of honeysuckle, and presently I asked if I might go into the garden a while; and cousin Agnes gave me leave, adding that I must soon go to bed, else I would be very tired next day. She noticed that I looked grave, and said that I must not dread being alone in the strange room, for it was so near her own. This was a great consolation; and after I had been told that the tide was in, and I must be careful not to go too near the river wall, I went out through the tall glass door, and slowly down the wide garden-walk, from which now and then narrower walks branched off at right angles. It was the pride of the place, this garden; and the box-borders especially were kept with great care. They had partly been trimmed that day; and the evening dampness brought out the faint, solemn odor of the leaves, which I never have noticed since without thinking of that night. The roses were in bloom, and the snowball-bushes were startlingly white, and there was a long border filled with lilies-of-the-valley. The other flowers of the season were all there and in blossom; yet I could see none well but the white ones, which looked like bits of snow and ice in the summer shadows,—ghostly flowers which one could see at night.

It was still in the garden, except once I heard a bird twitter sleepily, and once or twice a breeze came across the river, rustling the leaves a little. The small-paned windows glistened in the moonlight, and seemed like the eyes of the house watching me, the unknown new-comer.

For a while I wandered about, exploring the different paths, some of which were arched over by the tall lilacs, or by arbors where the grape-leaves did not seem fully grown. I wondered if my mother would miss me. It seemed impossible that I should have seen her only that morning; and suddenly I had a consciousness that she was thinking of me, and she seemed so close to me, that it would not be strange if she could hear what I said. And I called her twice softly; but the sound of my unanswered voice frightened me. I saw some round white flowers at my feet, looking up mockingly. The smell of the earth and the new grass seemed to smother me. I was afraid to be there all alone in the wide open air; and all the tall bushes that were so still around me took strange shapes, and seemed to be alive. I was so terribly far away from the mother whom I had called; the pleasure of my journey, and my coming to cousin Agnes, faded from my mind, and that indescribable feeling of hopelessness and dread, and of having made an irreparable mistake, came in its place. The thorns of a straying slender branch of a rose-bush caught my sleeve maliciously as I turned to hurry away, and then I caught sight of a person in the path just before me. It was such a relief to see some one, that I was not frightened when I saw that it must be Lady Ferry.

She was bent, but very tall and slender, and was walking slowly with a cane. Her head was covered with a great hood or wrapping of some kind, which she pushed back when she saw me. Some faint whitish figures on her dress looked like frost in the moonlight; and the dress itself was made of some strange stiff silk, which rustled softly like dry rushes and grasses in the autumn,—a rustling noise that carries a chill with it. She came close to me, a sorrowful little figure very dreary at heart, standing still as the flowers themselves; and for several minutes she did not speak, but watched me, until I began to be afraid of her. Then she held out her hand, which trembled as if it were trying to shake off its rings. "My dear," said she "I bid you welcome: I have known your father. I was told of your coming. Perhaps you will walk with me? I did not think to find you here alone." There was a fascinating sweetness in Madam's voice, and I at once turned to walk beside her, holding her hand fast, and keeping pace with her feeble steps. "Then you are not afraid of me?" asked the old lady, with a strange quiver in her voice. "It is a long time since I have seen a child."—"No," said I, "I am not afraid of you. I was frightened before I saw you, because I was all alone, and I wished I could see my father and mother;" and I hung my head so that my new friend could not see the tears in my eyes, for she watched me curiously. "All alone: that is like me," said she to herself. "All alone? a child is not all alone, but there is no one like me. I am something alone: there is nothing else of my fashion, a creature who lives forever!" and Lady Ferry sighed pitifully. Did she mean that she never was going to die like other people? But she was silent, and I did not dare to ask for any explanation as we walked back and forward. Her fingers kept moving round my wrist, smoothing it as if she liked to feel it, and to keep my hand in hers. It seemed to give her pleasure to have me with her, and I felt quite at my ease presently, and began to talk a little, assuring her that I did not mind having taken the journey of that day.

SARAH ORNE JEWETT

I had taken some long journeys: I had been to China once, and it took a great while to get there; but London was the nicest place I had ever seen; had Lady Ferry ever been in London? And I was surprised to hear her say drearily that she had been in London; she had been everywhere.

"Did you go to Westminster Abbey?" I asked, going on with the conversation childishly. "And did you see where Queen Elizabeth and Mary Queen of Scots are buried? Mamma had told me all about them."

"Buried, did you say? Are they dead too?" asked Madam eagerly. "Yes, indeed!" said I: "they have been dead a long time."—"Ah! I had forgotten," answered my strange companion. "Do you know of any one else who has died beside them? I have not heard of any one's dying and going home for so long! Once every one died but me—except some young people; and I do not know them."—"Why, every one must die," said I wonderingly. "There is a funeral somewhere every day, I suppose."—"Every one but me," Madam repeated sadly,—"every one but me, and I am alone."

Just now cousin Agnes came to the door, and called me. "Go in now, child," said Lady Ferry. "You may come and sit with me to-morrow if you choose." And I said good-night, while she turned, and went down the walk with feeble, lingering steps. She paced to and fro, as I often saw her afterwards, on the flag-stones; and some bats flew that way like ragged bits of darkness, holding somehow a spark of life. I watched her for a minute: she was like a ghost, I thought, but not a fearful ghost,—poor Lady Ferry!

"Have you had a pleasant walk?" asked cousin Matthew politely. "To-morrow I will give you a border for your own, and some plants for it, if you like gardening." I joyfully answered that I should like it very much, and so I began to feel already the pleasure of being in a real home, after the wandering life to which I had become used. I went close to cousin Agnes's chair to tell her confidentially that I had been walking with Madam in the garden, and she was very good to me, and asked me to come to sit with her the next day; but she said very odd things.

"You must not mind what she says," said cousin Agnes; "and I would never dispute with her, or even seem surprised, if I were you. It hurts and annoys her, and she soon forgets her strange fancies. I think you seem a very sensible little girl, and I have told you about this poor friend of ours as if you were older. But you understand, do you not?" And then she kissed me good-night, and I went up stairs, contented with her assurance that she would come to me before I went to sleep.

I found a pleasant-faced young girl busy putting away some of my clothing. I had seen her just after supper, and had fancied her very much, partly because she was not so old as the rest of the servants. We were friendly at once, and I found her very talkative; so finally I asked the question which was uppermost in my mind,—Did she know any thing about Madam?

"Lady Ferry, folks call her," said Martha, much interested. "I never have seen her close to, only from the other side of the garden, where she walks at night. She never goes out by day. Deborah waits upon her. I haven't been here long; but I have always heard about Madam, bless you! Folks tell all kinds of strange stories. She's fearful old, and there's many believes she never will die; and where she came from nobody knows. I've heard that her folks used to live here; but nobody can remember them, and she used to wander about; and once before she was here,—a good while ago; but this last time she come was nine years ago; one stormy night she came across the ferry, and scared them to death, looking in at the window like a ghost. She said she used to live here in Colonel Haverford's time. They saw she wasn't right in her head—the ferry-men did. But she came up to the house, and they let her in, and she went straight to the rooms in the north gable, and she never has gone away; it was in an awful storm she come, I've heard, and she looked just the same as she does now. There! I can't tell half the stories I've heard, and Deborah she most took my head off," said Martha, "because, when I first came, I was asking about her; and she said it was a sin to gossip about a harmless old creature whose mind was broke, but I guess most everybody thinks there's something mysterious. There's my grandmother—grandmother her mind is failing her; but she never had such ways! And then those clothes that my lady in the gable wears: they're unearthly looking; and I heard a woman say once, that they come out of a chest in the big garret, and they belonged to a Mistress Haverford who was hung for a witch, but there's no knowing that there is any truth in it." And Martha would have gone on with her stories, if just then we had not heard cousin Agnes's step on the stairway, and I hurried into bed.

But my bright eyes and excited look betrayed me. Cousin Agnes said she had hoped I would be asleep. And Martha said perhaps it was her fault; but I seemed wakeful, and she had talked with me a bit, to keep my spirits up, coming to a new, strange place. The apology was accepted, but Martha evidently had orders before I next saw her; for I never could get her to discuss Lady Ferry again; and she carefully told me that she should not have told those foolish stories, which were not true: but I knew that she still had her thoughts and suspicions as well as I. Once, when I asked her if Lady Ferry were Madam's real name, she answered with a guilty flush, "That's what the folks hereabout called her, because they didn't know any other at first." And this to me was another mystery. It was strongly impressed upon my mind that I must ask no questions, and that Madam was not to be discussed. No one distinctly forbade this; but I felt that it would not do. In every other way I was sure that I was allowed perfect liberty, so I soon ceased to puzzle myself or other people, and accepted Madam's presence as being perfectly explainable and natural,—just as the rest of the household did,—except once in a while something would set me at work romancing and wondering; and I read some stories in one of the books in the library,—of Peter Rugg the missing man, whom one may always meet riding from Salem to Boston in every storm, and of the Flying Dutchman and the Wandering Jew, and some terrible German stories of doomed people, and curses that were fulfilled. These made a great impression upon me; still I was not afraid, for all such things were far outside the boundaries of my safe little world; and I played by myself along the shore of the river and in the garden; and I had my lessons with cousin Agnes, and drives with cousin Matthew who was nearly always silent, but very kind to me. The house itself was an unfailing entertainment, with its many rooms, most of which were never occupied, and its quaint, sober furnishings, some of which were as old as the house itself. It was like a story-book; and no one minded my going where I pleased.

I missed my father and mother; but the only time I was really unhappy was the first morning after my arrival. Cousin Agnes was ill with a severe headache; cousin Matthew had ridden away to attend to some business; and, being left to myself, I had a most decided re-action from my unnaturally bright feelings of the day before. I began to write a letter to my mother; but unluckily I knew how many weeks must pass before she saw it, and it was useless to try to go on. I was lonely and homesick. The rain fell heavily, and the garden looked forlorn, and so unlike the enchanting moonlighted place where I had been in the evening! The walks were like little canals; and the rose-bushes looked wet and chilly, like some gay young lady who had been caught in the rain in party-dress. It was low-tide in the middle of the day, and the river-flats looked dismal. I fed cousin Agnes' flock of tame sparrows which came around the windows, and afterward some robins. I found some books and some candy which had come in my trunk, but my heart was very sad; and just after noon I was overjoyed when one of the servants told me that cousin Agnes would like to have me come to her room.

She was even kinder to me than she had been the night before; but she looked very ill, and at first I felt awkward, and did not know what to say. "I am afraid you have been very dull, dearie," said she, reaching out her hand to me. "I am sorry, and my headache hardly lets me think at all yet. But we will have better times to-morrow—both of us. You must ask for what you want; and you may come and spend this evening with me, for I shall be getting well then. It does me good to see your kind little face. Suppose you make Madam a call this afternoon. She told me last night that she wished for you, and I was so glad. Deborah will show you the way."

Deborah talked to me softly, out of deference to her mistress's headache, as we went along the crooked passages. "Don't you mind what Madam says, leastways don't you dispute her. She's got a funeral going on to-day;" and the grave woman smiled grimly at me. "It's curious she's taken to you so; for she never will see any strange folks. Nobody speaks to her about new folks lately," she added warningly, as she tapped at the door, and Madam asked, "Is it the child?" And Deborah lifted the latch. When I was fairly inside, my interest in life came back redoubled, and I was no longer sad, but looked round eagerly. Madam spoke to me, with her sweet old voice, in her courtly, quiet way, and stood looking out of the window.

There were two tall chests of drawers in the room, with shining brass handles and ornaments; and at one side, near the door, was a heavy mahogany table, on which I saw a large leather-covered Bible, a decanter of wine and some glasses, beside some cakes in a queer old tray. And there was no other furniture but a great number of chairs which seemed to have been collected from different parts of the house.

With these the room was almost filled, except an open space in the centre, toward which they all faced. One window was darkened; but Madam had pushed back the shutter of the other, and stood looking down at the garden. I waited for her to speak again after the first salutation, and presently she said I might be seated; and I took the nearest chair, and again waited her pleasure. It was gloomy enough, with the silence and the twilight in the room; and the rain and wind out of doors sounded louder than they had in cousin Agnes's room; but soon Lady Ferry came toward me.

"So you did not forget the old woman," said she, with a strange emphasis on the word old, as if that were her title and her chief characteristic. "And were not you afraid? I am glad it seemed worth while; for to-morrow would have been too late. You may like to remember by and by that you came. And my funeral is to be to-morrow, at last. You see the room is in readiness. You will care to be here, I hope. I would have ordered you some gloves if I had known; but these are all too large for your little hands. You shall have a ring; I will leave a command for that;" and Madam seated herself near me in a curious, high-backed chair. She was dressed that day in a maroon brocade, figured with bunches of dim pink flowers; and some of these flowers looked to me like wicked little faces. It was a mocking, silly creature that I saw at the side of every prim bouquet, and I looked at the faded little imps, until they seemed as much alive as Lady Ferry herself.

Her head nodded continually, as if it were keeping time to an inaudible tune, as she sat there stiffly erect. Her skin was pale and withered; and her cheeks were wrinkled in fine lines, like the crossings of a cobweb. Her eyes might once have been blue; but they had become nearly colorless, and, looking at her, one might easily imagine that she was blind. She had a singularly sweet smile, and a musical voice, which, though sad, had no trace of whining. If it had not been for her smile and her voice, I think madam would have been a terror to me. I noticed to-day, for the first time, a curious fragrance, which seemed to come from her old brocades and silks. It was very sweet, but unlike any thing I had ever known before; and it was by reason of this that afterward I often knew, with a little flutter at my heart, she had been in some other rooms of the great house beside her own. This perfume seemed to linger for a little while wherever she had been, and yet it was so faint! I used to go into the darkened chambers often, or even stay for a while by myself in the unoccupied lower rooms, and I would find this fragrance, and wonder if she were one of the oldtime fairies, who could vanish at their own will and pleasure, and wonder, too, why she had come to the room. But I never met her at all.

That first visit to her and the strange fancy she had about the funeral I have always remembered distinctly.

"I am glad you came," Madam repeated: "I was finding the day long. I am all ready, you see. I shall place a little chair which is in the next room, beside your cousin's seat for you. Mrs. Agnes is ill, I hear; but I think she will come to-morrow. Have you heard any one say if many guests are expected?"—"No, Madam," I answered, "no one has told me;" and just then the thought flitted through my head that she had said the evening before that all her friends were gone. Perhaps she expected their ghosts: that would not be stranger than all the rest.

The open space where Lady Ferry had left room for her coffin began to be a horror to me, and I wished Deborah would come back, or that my hostess would open the shutters; and it was a great relief when she rose and went into the adjoining room, bidding me follow her, and there opened a drawer containing some old jewelry; there were also some queer Chinese carvings, yellow with age,—just the things a child would enjoy. I looked at them delightedly. This was coming back to more familiar life; and I soon felt more at ease, and chattered to Lady Ferry of my own possessions, and some coveted treasures of my mother's, which were to be mine when I grew older.

Madam stood beside me patiently, and listened with a half smile to my whispered admiration. In the clearer light I could see her better, and she seemed older,—so old, so old! and my father's words came to me again. She had not changed since he was a boy; living on and on, and the 'horror of an endless life in this world!' And I remembered what Martha had said to me, and the consciousness of this mystery was a great weight upon me of a sudden. Why was she living so long? and what had happened to her? and how long could it be since she was a child?

There was something in her manner which made me behave, even in my pleasure, as if her imagined funeral were there in reality, and as if, in spite of my being amused and tearless, the solemn company of funeral guests already sat in the next room to us with bowed heads, and all the shadows in the world had assembled there materialized into the tangible form of crape. I opened and closed the boxes gently, and, when I had seen every thing, I looked up with a sigh to think that such a pleasure was ended, and asked if I might see them again some day. But the look in her face made me recollect myself, and my own grew crimson, for it seemed at that moment as real to me as to Lady Ferry herself that this was her last day of mortal life. She walked away, but presently came back, while I was wondering if I might not go, and opened the drawer again. It creaked, and the brass handles clacked in a startling way, and she took out a little case, and said I might keep it to remember her by. It held a little vinaigrette,—a tiny silver box with a gold one inside, in which I found a bit of fine sponge, dark brown with age, and still giving a faint, musty perfume and spiciness. The outside was rudely chased, and was worn as if it had been carried for years in somebody's pocket. It had a spring, the secret of which Lady Ferry showed me. I was delighted, and instinctively lifted my face to kiss her. She bent over me, and waited an instant for me to kiss her again. "Oh!" said she softly, "it is so long since a child has kissed me! I pray God not to leave you lingering like me, apart from all your kindred, and your life so long that you forget you ever were a child."— "I will kiss you every day," said I, and then again remembered that there were to be no more days according to her plan; but she did not seem to notice my mistake. And after this I used to go to see Madam often. For a time there was always the same gloom and hushed way of speaking, and the funeral services were to be on the morrow; but at last one day I found Deborah sedately putting the room in order, and Lady Ferry apologized for its being in such confusion; the idea of the funeral had utterly vanished, and I hurried to tell cousin Agnes with great satisfaction. I think that both she and cousin Matthew had a dislike for my being too much with Madam. I was kept out of doors as much as possible because it was much better for my health; and through the long summer days I strayed about wherever I chose. The country life was new and delightful to me. At home, Lady Ferry's vagaries were carelessly spoken of, and often smiled at; but I gained the idea that they disguised the truth, and were afraid of my being frightened. She often talked about persons who had been dead a very long time,—familiar characters in history, and, though cousin Agnes had said that she used to be fond of reading, it seemed to me that Madam might have known these men and women after all.

Once a middle-aged gentleman, an acquaintance of cousin Matthew's, came to pass a day and night at the ferry, and something happened then which seemed wonderful to me. It was early in the evening after tea, and we were in the parlor; from my seat by cousin Agnes I could look out into the garden, and presently, with the gathering darkness, came Lady Ferry, silent as a shadow herself, to walk to and fro on the flagstones. The windows were all open, and the guest had a clear, loud voice, and pleasant, hearty laugh; and, as he talked earnestly with cousin Matthew, I noticed that Lady Ferry stood still, as if she were listening. Then I was attracted by some story which was being told, and forgot her, but afterward turned with a start, feeling that there was some one watching; and, to my astonishment, Madam had come to the long window by which one went out to the garden. She stood there a moment, looking puzzled and wild; then she smiled, and, entering, walked in most stately fashion down the long room, toward the gentlemen, before whom she courtesied with great elegance, while the stranger stopped speaking, and looked at her with amazement, as he rose, and returned her greeting.

"My dear Captain Jack McAllister!" said she; "what a surprise! and are you not home soon from your voyage? This is indeed a pleasure." And Lady Ferry seated herself, motioning to him to take the chair beside her. She looked younger than I had ever seen her; a bright color came into her cheeks; and she talked so gayly, in such a different manner from her usual mournful gentleness. She must have been a beautiful woman; indeed she was that still.

"And did the good ship Starlight make a prosperous voyage? and had you many perils?—do you bring much news to us from the Spanish Main? We have missed you sadly at the assemblies; but there must be a dance in your honor. And your wife; is she not overjoyed at the sight of you? I think you have grown old and sedate since you went away. You do not look the gay sailor, or seem so light-hearted."

"I do not understand you, madam," said the stranger. "I am certainly John McAllister; but I am no captain, neither have I been at sea. Good God! is it my grandfather whom you confuse me with?" cried he. "He was Jack McAllister, and was lost at sea more than seventy years ago, while my own father was a baby. I am told that I am wonderfully like his portrait; but he was a younger man than I when he died. This is some masquerade."

Lady Ferry looked at him intently, but the light in her face was fast fading out. "Lost at sea,—lost at sea, were you, Jack McAllister, seventy years ago? I know nothing of years; one of my days is like another, and they are gray days, they creep away and hide, and sometimes one comes back to mock me. I have lived a thousand years; do you know it? Lost at sea—captain of the ship Starlight? Whom did you say?—Jack McAllister, yes, I knew him well—pardon me; good-evening;" and my lady rose, and with her head nodding and drooping, with a sorrowful, hunted look in her eyes, went out again into the shadows. She had had a flash of youth, the candle had blazed up brilliantly; but it went out again as suddenly, with flickering and smoke.

"I was startled when I saw her beside me," said Mr. McAllister. "Pray, who is she? she is like no one I have ever seen. I have been told that I am like my grandfather in looks and in voice; but it is years since I have seen any one who knew him well. And did you hear her speak of dancing? It is like seeing one who has risen from the dead. How old can she be?"—"I do not know," said cousin Matthew, "one can only guess at her age."—"Would not she come back? I should like to question her," asked the other. But cousin Matthew answered that she always refused to see strangers, and it would be no use to urge her, she would not answer him.

"Who is she? Is she any kin of yours?" asked Mr. McAllister.

"Oh, no!" said my cousin Agnes: "she has had no relatives since I have known her, and I think she has no friends now but ourselves. She has been with us a long time, and once before this house was her home for a time,—many years since. I suppose no one will ever know the whole history of her life; I wish often that she had power to tell it. We are glad to give shelter, and the little care she will accept, to the poor soul, God only knows where she has strayed and what she has seen. It is an enormous burden,—so long a life, and such a weight of memories; but I think it is seldom now that she feels its heaviness.—Go out to her, Marcia my dear, and see if she seems troubled. She always has a welcome for the child," cousin Agnes added, as I unwillingly went away.

I found Lady Ferry in the garden; I stole my hand into hers, and, after a few minutes of silence, I was not surprised to hear her say that they had killed the Queen of France, poor Marie Antoinette! she had known her well in her childhood, before she was a queen at all—"a sad fate, a sad fate," said Lady Ferry. We went far down the gardens and by the river-wall, and when we were again near the house, and could hear Mr. McAllister's voice as cheery as ever, madam took no notice of it. I had hoped she would go into the parlor again, and I wished over and over that I could have waited to hear the secrets which I was sure must have been told after cousin Agnes had sent me away.

One day I thought I had made a wonderful discovery. I was fond of reading, and found many books which interested me in cousin Matthew's fine library; but I took great pleasure also in hunting through a collection of old volumes which had been cast aside, either by him, or by some former owner of the house, and which were piled in a corner of the great garret. They were mostly yellow with age, and had dark brown leather or shabby paper bindings; the pictures in some were very amusing to me. I used often to find one which I appropriated and carried down stairs; and on this day I came upon a dusty, odd-shaped little book, for which I at once felt an affection. I looked at it a little. It seemed to be a journal, there were some stories of the Indians, and next I saw some reminiscences of the town of Boston, where, among other things, the author was told the marvellous story of one Mistress Honor Warburton, who was cursed, and doomed to live in this world forever. This was startling. I at once thought of Madam, and was reading on further to know the rest of the story, when some one called me, and I foolishly did not dare to carry my book with me. I was afraid I should not find it if I left it in sight; I saw an opening near me at the edge of the floor by the eaves, and I carefully laid my treasure inside. But, alas! I was not to be sure of its safe hiding-place in a way that I fancied, for the book fell down between the boarding of the thick walls, and I heard it knock as it fell, and knew by the sound that it must be out of reach. I grieved over this loss for a long time; and I felt that it had been most unkindly taken out of my hand. I wished heartily that I could know the rest of the story; and I tried to summon courage to ask Madam, when we were by ourselves, if she had heard of Honor Warburton, but something held me back. There were two other events just at this time which made this strange old friend of mine seem stranger than ever to me. I had a dream one night, which I took for a vision and a reality at the time. I thought I looked out of my window in the night, and there was bright moonlight, and I could see the other gable plainly; and I looked in at the windows of an unoccupied parlor which I never had seen open before, under Lady Ferry's own rooms. The shutters were pushed back, and there were candles burning; and I heard voices, and presently some tinkling music, like that of a harpsichord I had once heard in a very old house where I had been in England with my mother. I saw several couples go through with a slow, stately dance; and, when they stopped and seated themselves, I could hear their voices; but they spoke low, these midnight guests. I watched until the door was opened which led into the garden, and the company came out and stood for a few minutes on the little lawn, making their adieus, bowing low, and behaving with astonishing courtesy and elegance: finally the last good-nights were said, and they went away. Lady Ferry stood under the pointed porch, looking after them, and I could see her plainly in her brocade gown, with the impish flowers, a tall quaint cap, and a high lace frill at her throat, whiter than any lace I had ever seen, with a glitter on it; and there was a glitter on her face too. One of the other ladies was dressed in velvet, and I thought she looked beautiful: their eyes were all like sparks of fire. The gentlemen wore cloaks and ruffs, and high-peaked hats with wide brims, such as I had seen in some very old pictures which hung on the walls of the long west room. These were not pilgrims or Puritans, but gay gentlemen; and soon I heard the noise of their boats on the pebbles as they pushed off shore, and the splash of the oars in the water. Lady Ferry waved her hand, and went in at the door; and I found myself standing by the window in the chilly, cloudy night: the opposite gable, the garden, and the river, were indistinguishable in the darkness. I stole back to bed in an agony of fear; for it had been very real, that dream. I surely was at the window, for my hand had been on the sill when I waked; and I heard a church-bell ring two o'clock in a town far up the river. I never had heard this solemn bell before, and it seemed frightful; but I knew afterward that in the silence of a misty night the sound of it came down along the water.

In the morning I found that there had been a gale in the night; and cousin Matthew said at breakfast time that the tide had risen so that it had carried off two old boats that had been left on the shore to go to pieces. I sprang to the window, and sure enough they had disappeared. I had played in one of them the day before. Should I tell cousin Matthew what I had seen or dreamed? But I was too sure that he would only laugh at me; and yet I was none the less sure that those boats had carried passengers.

When I went out to the garden, I hurried to the porch, and saw, to my disappointment, that there were great spiders' webs in the corners of the door, and around the latch, and that it had not been opened since I was there before. But I saw something shining in the grass, and found it was a silver knee-buckle. It must have belonged to one of the ghostly guests, and my faith in them came back for a while, in spite of the cobwebs. By and by I bravely carried it up to Madam, and asked if it were hers. Sometimes she would not answer for a long time, when one rudely broke in upon her reveries, and she hesitated now, looking at me with singular earnestness. Deborah was in the room; and, when she saw the buckle, she quietly said that it had been on the window-ledge the day before, and must have slipped out. "I found it down by the doorstep in the grass," said I humbly; and then I offered Lady Ferry some strawberries which I had picked for her on a broad green leaf, and came away again.

A day or two after this, while my dream was still fresh in my mind, I went with Martha to her own home, which was a mile or two distant,—a comfortable farmhouse for those days, where I was always made welcome. The servants were all very kind to me: as I recall it now, they seemed to have a pity for me, because I was the only child perhaps. I was very happy, that is certain, and I enjoyed my childish amusements as heartily as if there were no unfathomable mysteries or perplexities or sorrows anywhere in the world.

I was sitting by the fireplace at Martha's, and her grandmother, who was very old, and who was fast losing her wits, had been talking to me about Madam. I do not remember what she said, at least, it made little impression; but her grandson, a worthless fellow, sauntered in, and began to tell a story of his own, hearing of whom we spoke. "I was coming home late last night," said he, "and, as I was in that dark place along by the Noroway pines, old Lady Ferry she went by me, and I was near scared to death. She looked fearful tall—towered way up above me. Her face was all lit up with blue light, and her feet didn't touch the ground. She wasn't taking steps, she wasn't walking, but movin' along like a sail-boat before the wind. I dodged behind some little birches, and I was scared she'd see me; but she went right out o' sight up the road. She ain't mortal."

"Don't scare the child with such foolishness," said his aunt disdainfully. "You'll be seein' worse things a-dancin' before your eyes than that poor, harmless old creatur' if you don't quit the ways you've been following lately. If that was last night, you were too drunk to see any thing;" and the fellow muttered, and went out, banging the door. But the story had been told, and I was stiffened and chilled with fright; and all the way home I was in terror, looking fearfully behind me again and again.

When I saw cousin Agnes, I felt safer, and since cousin Matthew was not at home, and we were alone, I could not resist telling her what I had heard. She listened to me kindly, and seemed so confident that my story was idle nonsense, that my fears were quieted. She talked to me until I no longer was a believer in there being any unhappy mystery or harmfulness; but I could not get over the fright, and I dreaded my lonely room, and I was glad enough when cousin Agnes, with her unfailing thoughtfulness, asked if I would like to have her come to sleep with me, and even went up stairs with me at my own early bedtime, saying that she should find it dull to sit all alone in the parlor. So I went to sleep, thinking of what I had heard, it is true, but no longer unhappy, because her dear arm was over me, and I was perfectly safe. I waked up for a little while in the night, and it was light in the room, so that I could see her face, fearless and sweet and sad, and I wondered, in my blessed sense of security, if she were ever afraid of any thing, and why I myself had been afraid of Lady Ferry.

I will not tell other stories: they are much alike, all my memories of those weeks and months at the ferry, and I have no wish to be wearisome. The last time I saw Madam she was standing in the garden door at dusk. I was going away before daylight in the morning. It was in the autumn: some dry leaves flittered about on the stone at her feet, and she was watching them. I said good-by again, and she did not answer me; but I think she knew I was going away, and I am sure she was sorry, for we had been a great deal together; and, child as I was, I thought to how many friends she must have had to say farewell.

Although I wished to see my father and mother, I cried as if my heart would break because I had to leave the ferry. The time spent there had been the happiest time of all my life, I think. I was old enough to enjoy, but not to suffer much, and there was singularly little to trouble one. I did not know that my life was ever to be different. I have learned, since those childish days, that one must battle against storms if one would reach the calm which is to follow them. I have learned also that anxiety, sorrow, and regret fall to the lot of every one, and that there is always underlying our lives, this mysterious and frightful element of existence; an uncertainty at times, though we do trust every thing to God. Under the best-loved and most beautiful face we know, there is hidden a skull as ghastly as that from which we turn aside with a shudder in the anatomist's cabinet. We smile, and are gay enough; God pity us! We try to forget our heart-aches and remorse. We even call our lives commonplace, and, bearing our own heaviest burdens silently, we try to keep the commandment, and to bear one another's also. There is One who knows: we look forward, as he means we shall, and there is always a hand ready to help us, though we reach out for it doubtfully in the dark.

For many years after this summer was over, I lived in a distant, foreign country; at last my father and I were to go back to America. Cousin Agnes and cousin Matthew, and my mother, were all long since dead, and I rarely thought of my childhood, for in an eventful and hurried life the present claims one almost wholly. We were travelling in Europe, and it happened that one day I was in a bookshop in

Amsterdam, waiting for an acquaintance whom I was to meet, and who was behind time.

The shop was a quaint place, and I amused myself by looking over an armful of old English books which a boy had thrown down near me, raising a cloud of dust which was plain evidence of their antiquity. I came to one, almost the last, which had a strangely familiar look, and I found that it was a copy of the same book which I had lost in the wall at the ferry. I bought it for a few coppers with the greatest satisfaction, and began at once to read it. It had been published in England early in the eighteenth century, and was written by one Mr. Thomas Highward of Chester,—a journal of his travels among some of the English colonists of North America, containing much curious and desirable knowledge, with some useful advice to those persons having intentions of emigrating. I looked at the prosy pages here and there, and finally found again those reminiscences of the town of Boston and the story of Mistress Honor Warburton, who was cursed, and doomed to live in this world to the end of time. She had lately been in Boston, but had disappeared again; she endeavored to disguise herself, and would not stay long in one place if she feared that her story was known, and that she was recognized. One Mr. Fleming, a man of good standing and repute, and an officer of Her Majesty Queen Anne, had sworn to Mr. Thomas Highward that his father, a person of great age, had once seen Mistress Warburton in his youth; that she then bore another name, but had the same appearance. "Not wishing to seem unduly credulous," said Mr. Highward, "I disputed this tale; but there was some considerable evidence in its favour, and at least this woman was of vast age, and was spoken of with extreme wonder by the town's folk."

I could not help thinking of my old childish suspicions of Lady Ferry, though I smiled at the folly of them and of this story more than once. I tried to remember if I had heard of her death; but I was still a child when my cousin Agnes had died. Had poor Lady Ferry survived her? and what could have become of her? I asked my father, but he could remember nothing, if indeed he ever had heard of her death at all. He spoke of our cousins' kindness to this forlorn soul, and that, learning her desolation and her piteous history (and being the more pitiful because of her shattered mind), when she had last wandered to their door, they had cared for the old gentlewoman to the end of her days—"for I do not think she can be living yet," said my father, with a merry twinkle in his eyes: "she must have been nearly a hundred years old when you saw her. She belonged to a fine old family which had gone to wreck and ruin. She strayed about for years, and it was a godsend to her to have found such a home in her last days."

That same summer we reached America, and for the first time since I had left it I went to the ferry. The house was still imposing, the prestige of the Haverford grandeur still lingered; but it looked forlorn and uncared for. It seemed very familiar; but the months I had spent there were so long ago, that they seemed almost to belong to another life. I sat alone on the doorstep for a long time, where I used often to watch for Lady Ferry; and forgotten thoughts and dreams of my childhood came back to me. The river was the only thing that seemed as young as ever. I looked in at some of the windows where the shutters were pushed back, and I walked about the garden, where I could hardly trace the walks, all overgrown with thick, short grass, though there were a few ragged lines of box, and some old rose-bushes; and I saw the very last of the flowers,—a bright red poppy, which had bloomed under a lilac-tree among the weeds.

Out beyond the garden, on a slope by the river, I saw the family burying-ground, and it was with a comfortable warmth at my heart that I stood inside the familiar old enclosure. There was my Lady Ferry's grave; there could be no mistake about it, and she was dead. I smiled at my satisfaction and at my foolish childish thoughts, and thanked God that there could be no truth in them, and that death comes surely,—say, rather, that the better life comes surely,—though it comes late.

The sad-looking, yellow-topped cypress, which only seems to feel quite at home in country burying-grounds, had kindly spread itself like a coverlet over the grave, which already looked like a very old grave; and the headstone was leaning a little, not to be out of the fashion of the rest. I traced again the words of old Colonel Haverford's pompous epitaph, and idly read some others. I remembered the old days so vividly there; I thought of my cousin Agnes, and wished that I could see her; and at last, as the daylight faded, I came away. When I crossed the river, the ferry-man looked at me wonderingly, for my eyes were filled with tears. Although we were in shadow on the water, the last red glow of the sun blazed on the high gable-windows, just as it did the first time I crossed over,—only a child then, with my life before me.

I asked the ferry-man some questions, but he could tell me nothing; he was a new-comer to that part of the country. He was sorry that the boat was not in better order; but there were almost never any passengers. The great house was out of repair: people would not live there, for they said it was haunted. Oh, yes! he had heard of Lady Ferry. She had lived to be very ancient; but she was dead.

"Yes," said I, "she is dead."

A Bit of Shore Life

I often think of a boy with whom I made friends last summer, during some idle, pleasant days that I spent by the sea. I was almost always out of doors, and I used to watch the boats go out and come in; and I had a hearty liking for the good-natured fishermen, who were lazy and busy by turns, who waited for the wind to change, and waited for the tide to turn, and waited for the fish to bite, and were always ready to gossip about the weather, and the fish, and the wonderful events that had befallen them and their friends.

Georgie was the only boy of whom I ever saw much at the shore. The few young people there were all went to school through the hot summer days at a little weather-beaten schoolhouse a mile or two inland. There were few houses to be seen, at any rate, and Georgie's house was the only one so close to the water. He looked already nothing but a fisherman; his clothes were covered with an oil-skin suit, which had evidently been awkwardly cut down for him from one of his father's, of whom he was a curious little likeness. I could hardly believe that he was twelve years old, he was so stunted and small; yet he was a strong little fellow; his hands were horny and hard from handling the clumsy oars, and his face was so brown and dry from the hot sun and chilly spray, that he looked even older when one came close to him. The first time I saw him was one evening just at night-fall. I was sitting on the pebbles, and he came down from the fish-house with some lobster-nets, and a bucket with some pieces of fish in it for bait, and put them into the stern of one of the boats which lay just at the edge of the rising tide. He looked at the clouds over the sea, and at the open sky overhead, in an old, wise way, and then, as if satisfied with the weather, began to push off his boat. It dragged on the pebbles; it was a heavy thing, and he could not get it far enough out to be floated by the low waves, so I went down to help him. He looked amazed that a girl should have thought of it, and as if he wished to ask me what good I supposed I could do, though I was twice his size. But the boat grated and slid down toward the sand, and I gave her a last push as the boy perched with one knee on her gunwale and let the other foot drag in the water for a minute. He was afloat after all; and he took the oars, and pulled manfully out toward the moorings, where the whale-boats and a sail-boat or two were swaying about in the wind, which was rising a little since the sun had set. He did not say a word to me, or I to him.

I watched him go out into the twilight,—such a little fellow, between those two great oars! But the boat could not drift or loiter with his steady stroke, and out he went, until I could only see the boat at last, lifting and sinking on the waves beyond the reef outside the moorings. I asked one of the fishermen whom I knew very well, "Who is that little fellow? Ought he to be out by himself, it is growing dark so fast?"

"Why, that's *Georgie!*" said my friend, with his grim smile. "Bless ye! he's like a duck; ye can't drown him. He won't be in until ten o'clock, like's not. He'll go way out to the far ledges when the tide covers them too deep where he is now. Lobsters he's after."

"Whose boy is he?" said I.

"Why, Andrer's, up here to the fish-house. *She's* dead, and him and the boy get along together somehow or 'nother. They've both got something saved up, and Andrer's a clever fellow; took it very hard, losing of his wife. I was telling of him the other day: 'Andrer,' says I, 'ye ought to look up somebody or 'nother, and not live this way. There's plenty o' smart, stirring women that would mend ye up, and cook for ye, and do well by ye.'—'No,' says he; 'I've hed my wife, and I've lost her.'—'Well, now,' says I, 'ye've shown respect, and there's the boy a-growin' up, and if either of you was took sick, why, here ye be.'—'Yes,' says he, 'here I be, sure enough;' and he drawed a long breath, 's if he felt bad; so that's all I said. But it's no way for a man to get along, and he ought to think of the boy. He owned a good house about half a mile up the road; but he moved right down here after she died, and his cousin took it, and it burnt up in the winter. Four year ago that was. I was down to the Georges Banks."

Some other men came down toward the water, and took a boat that was waiting, already fitted out with a trawl coiled in two tubs, and some hand-lines and bait for rock-cod and haddock, and my friend joined them; they were going out for a night's fishing. I watched them hoist the little sprit-sail, and drift a little until they caught the wind, and then I looked again for Georgie, whose boat was like a black spot on the water.

I knew him better soon after that. I used to go out with him for lobsters, or to catch cunners, and it was strange that he never had any cronies, and would hardly speak to the other children. He was very shy; but he had put all his heart into his work,—a man's hard work, which he had taken from choice. His father was kind to him; but he had a sorry home, and no mother,—the brave, fearless, steady little soul!

He looked forward to going one day (I hope that day has already dawned) to see the shipyards at a large seaport some twenty miles away. His face lit up when he told me of it, as some other child's would who had been promised a day in fairy-land. And he confided to me that he thought he should go to the Banks that coming winter. "But it's so cold!" said I: "should you really like it?"—"Cold!" said Georgie. "Ho! rest of the men never froze." That was it,—the "rest of the men;" and he would work until he dropped, or tend a line until his fingers froze, for the sake of that likeness,—the grave, slow little man, who has so much business with the sea, and who trusts himself with touching confidence to its treacherous keeping and favor.

Andrew West, Georgie's father, was almost as silent as his son at first, but it was not long before we were very good friends, and I went out with him at four o'clock one morning, to see him set his trawl. I remember there was a thin mist over the sea, and the air was almost chilly; but, as the sun came up, it changed the color of every thing to the most exquisite pink,—the smooth, slow waves, and the mist that blew over them as if it were a cloud that had fallen down out of the sky. The world just then was like the hollow of a great pink sea-shell; and we could only hear the noise of it, the dull sound of the waves among the outer ledges.

We had to drift about for an hour or two when the trawl was set; and after a while the fog shut down again gray and close, so we could not see either the sun or the shore. We were a little more than four miles out, and we had put out more than half a mile of lines. It is very interesting to see the different fish that come up on the hooks,—worthless sculpin and dog-fish, and good rock-cod and haddock, and curious stray creatures which often even the fisherman do not know. We had capital good luck that morning, and Georgie and Andrew and I were all pleased. I had a hand-line, and was fishing part of the time, and Georgie thought very well of me when he found I was not afraid of a big fish, and, besides that, I had taken the oars while he tended the sail, though there was hardly wind enough to make it worth his while. It was about eight o'clock when we came in, and there was a horse and wagon standing near the landing; and we saw a woman come out of Andrew's little house. "There's your aunt Hannah a'ready," said he to Georgie; and presently she came down the pebbles to meet the boat, looking at me with much wonder as I jumped ashore.

"I sh'd think you might a' cleaned up your boat, Andrer, if you was going to take ladies out," said she graciously. And the fisherman rejoined, that perhaps she would have thought it looked better when it went out than it did then; he never had got a better fare o' fish unless the trawls had been set over night.

There certainly had been a good haul; and, when Andrew carefully put those I had caught with the hand-line by themselves, I asked his sister to take them, if she liked. "Bless you!" said she, much pleased, "we couldn't eat one o' them big rock-cod in a week. I'll take a little ha'dick, if Andrer 'll pick me one out."

She was a tall, large woman, who had a direct, business-like manner,—what the country people would call a master smart woman, or a regular driver,—and I liked her. She said something to her brother about some clothes she had been making for him or for Georgie, and I went off to the house where I was boarding for my breakfast. I was hungry enough, since I had had only a hurried lunch a good while before sunrise. I came back late in the morning, and found that Georgie's aunt was just going away. I think my friends must have spoken well of me, for she came out to meet me as I nodded in going by, and said, "I suppose ye drive about some? We should be pleased to have ye come up to see us. We live right 'mongst the woods; it ain't much of a place to ask anybody to." And she added that she might have done a good deal better for herself to have staid off. But there! they had the place, and she supposed she and Cynthy had done as well there as anywhere. Cynthy—well, she wasn't one of your pushing kind; but I should have some flowers, and perhaps it would be a change for me. I thanked her, and said I should be delighted to go. Georgie and I would make her a call together some afternoon when he wasn't busy; and Georgie actually smiled when I looked at him, and said, "All right," and then hurried off down the shore. "Ain't he an odd boy?" said Miss Hannah West, with a shadow of disapproval in her face. "But he's just like his father and grandfather before him; you wouldn't think they had no gratitude nor feelin', but I s'pose they have. They used to say my father never'd forgit a friend, or forgive an enemy. Well, I'm much obliged to you, I'm sure, for taking an interest in the boy." I said I liked him; I only wished I could do something for him. And then she said good-day, and drove off. I felt as if we were already good friends. "I'm much obliged for the fish," she turned round to say to me again, as she went away.

One morning, not very long afterward, I asked Georgie if he could possibly leave his business that afternoon, and he gravely answered me that he could get away just as well as not, for the tide would not be right for lobsters until after supper.

"I should like to go up and see your aunt," said I. "You know she asked me to come the other day when she was here."

"I'd like to go," said Georgie sedately. "Father was going up this week; but the mackerel struck in, and we couldn't leave. But it's better'n six miles up there."

"That's not far," said I. "I'm going to have Captain Donnell's horse and wagon;" and Georgie looked much interested.

I wondered if he would wear his oil-skin suit; but I was much amazed, and my heart was touched, at seeing how hard he had tried to put himself in trim for the visit. He had on his best jacket and trousers (which might have been most boys' worst), and a clean calico shirt; and he had scrubbed his freckled, honest little face and his hard little hands, until they were as clean as possible; and either he or his father had cut his hair. I should think it had been done with a knife, and it looked as if a rat had gnawed it. He had such a holiday air! He really looked very well; but still, if I were to have a picture of Georgie, it should be in the oil-skin fishing-suit. He had gone out to his box, which was anchored a little way out in the cove, and had chosen two fine lobsters which he had tied together with a bit of fish-line. They were lazily moving their claws and feelers; and his father, who had come in with his boat not long before, added from his fare of fish three plump mackerel.

"They're always glad to get new fish," said he. "The girls can't abide a fish that's corned, and I haven't had a chance to send 'em up any mackerel before. Ye see, they live on a cross-road, and the fish-carts don't go by." And I told him I was very glad to carry them, or any thing else he would like to send. "Mind your manners, now, Georgie," said he, "and don't be forrard. You might split up some kindlin's for y'r aunts, and do whatever they want of ye. Boys ain't made just to look at, so ye be handy, will ye?" And Georgie nodded solemnly. They seemed very fond of each other, and I looked back some time afterward to see the fisherman still standing there to watch his boy. He was used to his being out at sea alone for hours; but this might be a great risk to let him go off inland to stay all the afternoon.

The road crossed the salt-marshes for the first mile, and, when we had struck the higher land, we soon entered the pine-woods, which cover a great part of that country. It had been raining in the morning for a little while; and the trunks of the trees were still damp, and the underbrush was shining wet, and sent out a sweet, fresh smell. I spoke of it, and Georgie told me that sometimes this fragrance blew far out to sea, and then you knew the wind was north-west.

"There's the big pine you sight Minister's Ledge by," said he, "when that comes in range over the white schoolhouse, about two miles out."

The lobsters were clashing their pegged claws together in the back of the wagon, and Georgie sometimes looked over at them to be sure they were all right. Of course I had given him the reins when we first started, and he was delighted because we saw some squirrels, and even a rabbit, which scurried across the road as if I had been a fiery dragon, and Georgie something worse.

We presently came in sight of a house close by the road,—an old-looking place, with a ledgy, forlorn field stretching out behind it toward some low woods. There were high white-birch poles holding up thick tangles of hop-vines, and at the side there were sunflowers straggling about as if they had come up from seed scattered by the wind. Some of them were close together, as if they were whispering to each other; and their big, yellow faces were all turned toward the front of the house, where people were already collected as if there were a funeral.

"It's the auction," said Georgie with great satisfaction. "I heard 'em talking about it down at the shore this morning. There's 'Lisha Downs now. He started off just before we did. That's his fish-cart over by the well."

"What is going to be sold?" said I.

"All the stuff," said Georgie, as if he were much pleased. "She's going off up to Boston with her son."

"I think we had better stop," said I, for I saw Mrs. 'Lisha Downs, who was one of my acquaintances at the shore, and I wished to see what was going on, besides giving Georgie a chance at the festivities. So we tied the horse, and went toward the house, and I found several people whom I knew a little. Mrs. Downs shook hands with me as formally as if we had not talked for some time as I went by her house to the shore, just after breakfast. She presented me to several of her friends with whom she had been talking as I came up. "Let me make you acquainted," she said; and every time I bowed she bowed too, unconsciously, and seemed a little ill at ease and embarrassed, but luckily the ceremony was soon over. "I thought I would stop for a few minutes," said I by way of apology. "I didn't know why the people were here until Georgie told me."

"She's going to move up to Boston 'long of her son," said one of the women, who looked very pleasant and very tired. "I think myself it's a bad plan to pull old folks up by the roots. There's a niece o' hers that would have been glad to stop with her, and do for the old lady. But John, he's very high-handed, and wants it his way, and he says his mother sha'n't live in no such a place as this. He makes a sight o' money. He's got out a patent, and they say he's just bought a new house that cost him eleven thousand dollars. But old Mis' Wallis, she's wonted here; and she was telling of me yesterday she was only going to please John. He says he wants her up there, where she'll be more comfortable, and see something."

"He means well," said another woman whom I did not know; "but folks about here never thought no great of his judgment. He's put up some splendid stones in the burying-lot to his father and his sister Miranda that died. I used to go to school 'long of Miranda. She'd have been pleased to go to Boston; she was that kind. But there! mother was saying last night, what if his business took a turn, and he lost every thing! Mother's took it dreadfully to heart; she and Mis' Wallis was always mates as long ago as they can recollect."

It was evident that the old widow was both pitied and envied by her friends on account of her bettered fortunes, and they came up to speak to her with more or less seriousness, as befitted the occasion. She looked at me with great curiosity, but Mrs. Downs told her who I was, and I had a sudden instinct to say how sorry I was for her, but I was afraid it might appear intrusive on so short an acquaintance. She was a thin old soul who looked as if she had had a good deal of trouble in her day, and as if she had been very poor and very anxious. "Yes," said she to some one who had come from a distance, "it does come hard to go off. Home is home, and I seem to hate to sell off my things; but I suppose they would look queer up to Boston. John Bays says I won't have no idea of the house until I see it;" and she looked proud and important for a minute, but, as some one brought an old chair out at the door, her face fell again. "Oh, dear!" said she, "I should like to keep that! it belonged to my mother. It's most wore out anyway. I guess I'll let somebody keep it for me;" and she hurried off despairingly to find her son, while we went into the house.

There is so little to interest the people who live on those quiet, secluded farms, that an event of this kind gives great pleasure. I know they have not done talking yet about the sale, of the bargains that were made, or the goods that brought more than they were worth. And then the women had the chance of going all about the house, and committing every detail of its furnishings to their tenacious memories. It is a curiosity one grows more and more willing to pardon, for there is so little to amuse them in every-day life. I wonder if any one has not often been struck, as I have, by the sadness and hopelessness which seems to overshadow many of the people who live on the lonely farms in the outskirts of small New-England villages. It is most noticeable among the elderly women. Their talk is very cheerless, and they have a morbid interest in sicknesses and deaths; they tell each other long stories about such things; they are very forlorn; they dwell persistently upon any troubles which they have; and their petty disputes with each other have a tragic hold upon their thoughts, sometimes being handed down from one generation to the next. Is it because their world is so small, and life affords so little amusement and pleasure, and is at best such a dreary round of the dullest housekeeping? There is a lack of real merriment, and the fun is an odd, rough way of joking; it is a stupid, heavy sort of fun, though there is much of a certain quaint humor, and once in a while a flash of wit. I came upon a short, stout old sister in one room, making all the effort she possibly could to see what was on the upper shelves of a closet. We were the only persons there, and she looked longingly at a convenient chair, and I know she wished I would go away. But my heart suddenly went out toward an old dark-green Delft bowl which I saw, and I asked her if she would be kind enough to let me take it, as if I thought she were there for the purpose. "I'll bring you a chair," said I; and she said, "Certain, dear." And I helped her up, and I'm sure she had the good look she had coveted while I took the bowl to the window. It was badly cracked, and had been mended with putty; but the rich, dull color of it was exquisite. One often comes across a beautiful old stray bit of china in such a place as this, and I imagined it filled with apple-blossoms or wild roses. Mrs. Wallis wished to give it to me, she said it wasn't good for any thing; and, finding she did not care for it, I bought it; and now it is perched high in my room, with the cracks discreetly turned to the wall. "Seems to me she never had thrown away nothing," said my friend, whom I found still standing on the chair when I came back. "Here's some pieces of a pitcher: I wonder when she broke it! I've heard her say it was one her grandmother give her, though. The old lady bought it to a vandoo down at old Mis' Walton Peters's after she died, so Mis' Wallis said. I guess I'll speak to her, and see if she wants every thing sold that's here."

There was a very great pathos to me about this old home. It must have been a hard place to get a living in, both for men and women, with its wretched farming-land, and the house itself so cold and thin and worn out. I could understand that the son was in a hurry to get his mother away from it. I was sure that the boyhood he had spent there must have been uncomfortable, and that he did not look back to it with much pleasure. There is an immense contrast between even a moderately comfortable city house and such a place as this. No wonder that he remembered the bitter cold mornings, the frost and chill, and the dark, and the hard work, and wished his mother to leave them all behind, as he had done! He did not care for the few plain bits of furniture; why should he? and he had been away so long, that he had lost his interest in the neighbors. Perhaps this might come back to him again as he grew older; but now he moved about among them, in his handsome but somewhat flashy clothes, with a look that told me he felt conscious of his superior station in life. I did not altogether like his looks, though somebody said admiringly, as he went by, "They say he's worth as much as thirty thousand dollars a'ready. He's smart as a whip." But, while I did not wonder at the son's wishing his mother to go away, I also did not wonder at her being unwilling to leave the dull little house where she had spent so much of her life. I was afraid no other house in the world would ever seem like home to her: she was a part of the old place; she had worn the doors smooth by the touch of her hands, and she had scrubbed the floors, and walked over them, until the knots stood up high in the pine boards. The old clock had been unscrewed from the wall, and stood on a table; and when I heard its loud and anxious tick, my first thought was one of pity for the poor thing, for fear it might be homesick, like its mistress. When I went out again, I was very sorry for old Mrs. Wallis; she looked so worried and excited, and as if this new turn of affairs in her life was too strange and unnatural; it bewildered her, and she could not understand it; she only knew every thing was going to be different.

Georgie was by himself, as usual, looking grave and intent. He had gone aloft on the wheel of a clumsy great ox-cart in which some of the men had come to the auction, and he was looking over people's heads, and seeing every thing that was sold. I saw he was not ready to come away, so I was not in a hurry. I heard Mrs. Wallis say to one of her friends, "You just go in and take that rug with the flowers on't, and go and put it in your wagon. It's right beside my chist that's packed ready to go. John told me to give away any thing I had a mind to. He don't care nothing about the money. I hooked that rug four year ago; it's most new; the red of the roses was made out of a dress of Miranda's. I kept it a good while after she died; but it was no use to let it lay. I've given a good deal to my sister Stiles: she was over here helping me yesterday. There! it's all come upon me so sudden! I s'pose I shall wish, after I get away, that I had done things different; but, after I knew the farm was goin' to be sold, I didn't seem to realize I was goin' to break up, until John came, day before yesterday."

She was very friendly with me, when I said I should think she would be sorry to go away; but she seemed glad to find I had been in Boston a great deal, and that I was not at all unhappy there. "But I suppose you have folks there," said she, "though I never supposed they was so sociable as they be here, and I ain't one that's easy to make acquaintance. It's different with young folks; and then in case o'sickness I should hate to have strange folks round me. It seems as if I never set so much by the old place as I do now I'm goin' away. I used to wish 'he' would sell, and move over to the Port, it was such hard work getting along when the child'n was small. And there's one of my boys that run away to sea, and never was heard from. I've always thought he might come back, though everybody give him up years ago. I can't help thinking what if he should come back, and find I wa'n't here! There! I'm glad to please John: he sets everything by me, and I s'pose he thinks he's going to make a spry young woman of me. Well, it's natural. Every thing looks fair to him, and he thinks he can have the world just as he wants it; but *I* know it's a world o' change,—a world o' change and loss. And, you see, I shall have to go to a strange meetin' up there.—Why, Mis' Sands! I am pleased to see you. How did you get word?" And then Mrs. Wallis made another careful apology for moving away. She seemed to be so afraid some one would think she had not been satisfied with the neighborhood.

The auctioneer was a disagreeable-looking man, with a most unpleasant voice, which gave me a sense of discomfort, the little old house and its surroundings seemed so grave and silent and lonely. It was like having all the noise and confusion on a Sunday. The house was so shut in by the trees, that the only outlook to the world beyond was a narrow gap in the pines, through which one could see the sea, bright, blue and warm with sunshine, that summer day.

There was something wistful about the place, as there must have been about the people who had lived there; yet, hungry and unsatisfied as her life might have been in many ways, the poor old woman dreaded the change.

The thought flashed through my mind that we all have more or less of this same feeling about leaving this world for a better one. We have the certainty that we shall be a great deal happier in heaven; but we cling despairingly to the familiar things of this life. God pity the people who find it so hard to believe what he says, and who are afraid to die, and are afraid of the things they do not understand! I kept thinking over and over of what Mrs. Wallis had said: 'A world of change and loss!' What should we do if we did not have God's love to make up for it, and if we did not know something of heaven already?

It seemed very doleful that everybody should look on the dark side of the Widow Wallis's flitting, and I tried to suggest to her some of the pleasures and advantages of it, once when I had a chance. And indeed she was proud enough to be going away with her rich son; it was not like selling her goods because she was too poor to keep the old home any longer. I hoped the son would always be prosperous, and that the son's wife would always be kind, and not be ashamed of her, or think she was in the way. But I am afraid it may be a somewhat uneasy idleness, and that there will not be much beside her knitting-work to remind her of the old routine. She will even miss going back and forward from the old well in storm and sunshine; she will miss looking after the chickens, and her slow walks about the little place, or out to a neighbor's for a bit of gossip, with the old brown checked handkerchief over her head; and when the few homely, faithful old flowers come up next year by the doorstep, there will be nobody to care any thing about them.

I said good-by, and got into the wagon, and Georgie clambered in after me with a look of great importance, and we drove away. He was very talkative; the unusual excitement of the day was not without its effect. He had a good deal to tell me about the people I had seen, though I had to ask a good many questions.

"Who was the thin old fellow, with the black coat, faded yellow-green on the shoulders, who was talking to Skipper Downs about the dog-fish?"

"That's old Cap'n Abiah Lane," said Georgie; "lives over toward Little Beach,—him that was cast away in the fog in a dory down to the Banks once; like to have starved to death before he got picked up. I've heard him tell all about it. Don't look as if he'd ever had enough to eat since!" said the boy grimly. "He used to come over a good deal last winter, and go out after cod 'long o' father and me. His boats all went adrift in the big storm in November, and he never heard nothing about 'em; guess they got stove against the rocks."

We had still more than three miles to drive over a lonely part of the road, where there was scarcely a house, and where the woods had been cut off more or less, so there was nothing to be seen but the uneven ground, which was not fit for even a pasture yet. But it was not without a beauty of its own; for the little hills and hollows were covered thick with brakes and ferns and bushes, and in the swamps the cat-tails and all the rushes were growing in stiff and stately ranks, so green and tall; while the birds flew up, or skimmed across them as we went by. It was like a town of birds, there were so many. It is strange how one is always coming upon families and neighborhoods of wild creatures in the unsettled country places; it is so much like one's going on longer journeys about the world, and finding town after town with its own interests, each so sufficient for itself.

We struck the edge of the farming-land again, after a while, and I saw three great pines that had been born to good luck in this world, since they had sprouted in good soil, and had been left to grow as fast as they pleased. They lifted their heads proudly against the blue sky, these rich trees, and I admired them as much as they could have expected. They must have been a landmark for many miles to the westward, for they grew on high land, and they could pity, from a distance, any number of their poor relations who were just able to keep body and soul together, and had grown up thin and hungry in crowded woods. But, though their lower branches might snap and crackle at a touch, their tops were brave and green, and they kept up appearances, at any rate; these poorer pines.

Georgie pointed out his aunts' house to me, after a while. It was not half so forlorn-looking as the others, for there were so many flowers in bloom about it of the gayest kind, and a little yellow-and-white dog came down the road to bark at us; but his manner was such that it seemed like an unusually cordial welcome rather than an indignant repulse. I noticed four jolly old apple-trees near by, which looked as if they might be the last of a once flourishing orchard. They were standing in a row, in exactly the same position, with their heads thrown gayly back, as if they were all dancing in an old-fashioned reel; and, after the forward and back, one might expect them to turn partners gallantly. I laughed aloud when I caught sight of them: there was something very funny in their looks, so jovial and whole-hearted, with a sober, cheerful pleasure, as if they gave their whole minds to it. It was like some old gentlemen and ladies who catch the spirit of the thing, and dance with the rest at a Christmas party.

Miss Hannah West first looked out of the window, and then came to meet us, looking as if she were glad to see us. Georgie had nothing whatever to say; but, after I had followed his aunt into the house, he began to work like a beaver at once, as if it were any thing but a friendly visit that could be given up to such trifles as conversation, or as if he were any thing but a boy. He brought the fish and lobsters into the outer kitchen, though I was afraid our loitering at the auction must have cost them their first freshness; and then he carried the axe to the wood-pile, and began to chop up the small white-pine sticks and brush which form the summer fire-wood at the farm-houses,—crow-sticks and underbrush, a good deal of it,—but it makes a hot little blaze while it lasts.

I had not seen Miss Cynthia West, the younger sister, before, and I found the two women very unlike. Miss Hannah was evidently the capable business-member of the household, and she had a loud voice, and went about as if she were in a hurry. Poor Cynthia! I saw at first that she was one of the faded-looking country-women who have a hard time, and who, if they had grown up in the midst of a more luxurious way of living, would have been frail and delicate and refined, and entirely lady-like. But, as it was, she was somewhat in the shadow of her sister, and felt as if she were not of very much use or consequence in the world, I have no doubt. She showed me some pretty picture-frames she had made out of pine-cones and hemlock-cones and alder-burs; but her chief glory and pride was a silly little model of a house, in perforated card-board, which she had cut and worked after a pattern that came in a magazine. It must have cost her a great deal of work; but it partly satisfied her great longing for pretty things, and for the daintiness and art that she had an instinct toward, and never had known. It stood on the best-room table, with a few books, which I suppose she had read over and over again; and in the room, beside, were green paper curtains with a landscape on the outside, and some chairs ranged stiffly against the walls, some shells, and an ostrich's egg, with a ship drawn on it, on the mantel-shelf, and ever so many rugs on the floor, of most ambitious designs, which they had made in winter. I know the making of them had been a great pleasure to Miss Cynthia, and I was sure it was she who had taken care of the garden, and was always at much pains to get seeds and slips in the spring.

She told me how much they had wished that Georgie had come to live with them after his mother died. It would have been very handy for them to have him in winter too; but it was no use trying to get him away from his father; and neither of them were contented if they were out of sight of the sea. "He's a dreadful odd boy, and so old for his years. Hannah, she says he's older now than I be," and she blushed a little as she looked up at me; while for a moment the tears came into my eyes, as I thought of this poor, plain woman, who had such a capacity for enjoyment, and whose life had been so dull, and far apart from the pleasures and satisfactions which had made so much of my own life. It seemed to me as if I had had a great deal more than I deserved, while this poor soul was almost beggared. I seemed to know all about her life in a flash, and pitied her from the bottom of my heart. Yet I suppose she would not have changed places with me for any thing, or with anybody else, for that matter.

Miss Cynthia had a good deal to say about her mother, who had been a schoolmate of Mrs. Wallis's—I had been telling them what I could about the auction. She told me that she had died the spring before, and said how much they missed her; and Hannah broke in upon her regrets in her brusque, downright way: "I should have liked to kep' her if she'd lived to be a hundred, but I don't wish her back. She'd had considerable many strokes, and she couldn't help herself much of any. She'd got to be rising eighty, and her mind was a good deal broke," she added conclusively, after a short silence; while Cynthia looked sorrowfully out of the window, and we heard the sound of Georgie's axe at the other side of the house, and the wild, sweet whistle of a bird that flew overhead. I suppose one of the sisters was just as sorry as the other in reality.

"Now I want you and Georgie to stop and have some tea. I'll get it good and early," said Hannah, starting suddenly from her chair, and beginning to bustle about again, after she had asked me about some people at home whom she knew. "Cynthy! Perhaps she'd like to walk round out doors a spell. It's breezing up, and it'll be cooler than it is in the house.—No: you needn't think I shall be put out by your stopping; but you'll have to take us just as we be. Georgie always calculates to stop when he comes up. I guess he's made off for the woods. I see him go across the lot a few minutes ago."

So Cynthia put on a discouraged-looking gingham sun-bonnet, which drooped over her face, and gave her a more appealing look than ever, and we went over to the pine-woods, which were beautiful that day. She showed me a little waterfall made by a brook that came over a high ledge of rock covered with moss, and here and there tufts of fresh green ferns. It grew late in the afternoon, and it was pleasant there in the shade, with the noise of the brook and the wind in the pines, that sounded like the sea. The wood-thrushes began to sing,—and who could have better music?

Miss Cynthia told me that it always made her think of once when she was a little girl to hear the thrushes. She had run away, and fallen into the ma'sh; and her mother had sent her to bed quick as she got home, though it was only four o'clock. And she was so ashamed, because there was company there,—some of her father's folks from over to Eliot; and then she heard the thrushes begin to call after a while, and she thought they were talking about her, and they knew she had been whipped and sent to bed. "I'd been gone all day since morning. I had a great way of straying off in the woods," said she. "I suppose mother was put to it when she see me coming in, all bog-mud, right before the company."

We came by my friends, the apple-trees, on our return, and I saw a row of old-fashioned square bee-hives near them, which I had not noticed before. Miss Cynthia told me that the bee money was always hers; but she lost a good many swarms on account of the woods being so near, and they had a trick of swarming Sundays, after she'd gone to meeting; and, besides, the miller-bugs spoilt 'em; and some years they didn't make enough honey to live on, so she didn't get any at all. I saw some bits of black cloth fluttering over the little doors where the bees went in and out, and the sight touched me strangely. I did not know that the old custom still lingered of putting the hives in mourning, and telling the bees when there had been a death in the family, so they would not fly away. I said, half to myself, a line or two from Whittier's poem, which I always thought one of the loveliest in the world, and this seemed almost the realization of it. Miss Cynthia asked me wistfully, "Is that in a book?" I told her yes, and that she should have it next time I came up, or had a chance of sending it. "I've seen a good many pieces of poetry that Mr. Whittier wrote," said she. "I've got some that I cut out of the paper a good while ago. I think every thing of 'em."

"I put the black on the hives myself," said she. "It was for mother, you know. She did it when father died. But when my brother was lost, we didn't, because we never knew just when it was; the schooner was missing, and it was a good while before they give her up."

"I wish we had some neighbors in sight," said she once. "I'd like to see a light when I look out after dark. Now, at my aunt's, over to Eliot, the house stands high, and when it's coming dark you can see all the folks lighting up. It seems real sociable."

We lingered a little while under the apple-trees, and watched the wise little bees go and come; and Miss Cynthia told me how much Georgie was like his grandfather, who was so steady and quiet, and always right after his business. "He never was ugly to us, as I know of," said she; "but I was always sort of 'fraid of father. Hannah, she used to talk to him free's she would to me; and he thought, 's long's Hannah did any thing, it was all right. I always held by my mother the most; and when father was took sick,—that was in the winter,—I sent right off for Hannah to come home. I used to be scared to death, when he'd want any thing done, for fear I shouldn't do it right. Mother, she'd had a fall, and couldn't get about very well. Hannah had good advantages. She went off keeping school when she wasn't but seventeen, and she saved up some money, and boarded over to the Port after a while, and learned the tailoress trade. She was always called very smart,—you see she's got ways different from me; and she was over to the Port several winters. She never said a word about it, but there was a young man over there that wanted to keep company with her. He was going out first mate of a new ship that was building. But, when she got word from me about father, she come right home, and that was the end of it. It seemed to be a pity. I used to think perhaps he'd come and see her some time, between voyages, and that he'd get to be cap'n, and they'd go off and take me with 'em. I always wanted to see something of the world. I never have been but dreadful little ways from home. I used to wish I could keep school; and once my uncle was agent for his district, and he said I could have a chance; but the folks laughed to think o' me keeping school, and I never said any thing more about it. But you see it might 'a' led to something. I always wished I could go to Boston. I suppose you've been there? There! I couldn't live out o' sight o' the woods, I don't believe."

"I can understand that," said I, and half with a wish to show her I had some troubles, though I had so many pleasures that she did not, I told her that the woods I loved best had all been cut down the winter before. I had played under the great pines when I was a child, and I had spent many a long afternoon under them since. There never will be such trees for me any more in the world. I knew where the flowers grew under them, and where the ferns were greenest, and it was as much home to me as my own house. They grew on the side of a hill, and the sun always shone through the tops of the trees as it went down, while below it was all in shadow—and I had been there with so many dear friends who have died, or who are very far away. I told Miss Cynthia, what I never had told anybody else, that I loved those trees so much that I went over the hill on the frozen snow to see them one sunny winter afternoon, to say good-by, as if I were sure they could hear me, and looked back again and again, as I came away, to be sure I should remember how they looked. And it seemed as if they knew as well as I that it was the last time, and they were going to be cut down. It was a Sunday afternoon, and I was all alone, and the farewell was a reality and a sad thing to me. It was saying good-by to a great deal besides the pines themselves.

We stopped a while in the little garden, where Miss Cynthia gave me some magnificent big marigolds to put away for seed, and was much pleased because I was so delighted with her flowers. It was a gorgeous little garden to look at, with its red poppies, and blue larkspur, and yellow marigolds, and old-fashioned sweet, straying things,—all growing together in a tangle of which my friend seemed ashamed. She told me that it looked as ordered as could be, until the things begun to grow so fast she couldn't do any thing with 'em. She was very proud of one little pink-and-white verbena which somebody had given her. It was not growing very well; but it had not disappointed her about blooming.

Georgie had come back from his ramble some time before. He had cracked the lobster which Miss Hannah had promptly put on to boil, and I saw the old gray cat having a capital lunch off the shells; while the horse looked meeker than ever, with his headstall thrown back on his shoulders, eating his supper of hay by the fence; for Miss Hannah was a hospitable soul. She was tramping about in the house, getting supper, and we went in to find the table already pulled out into the floor. So Miss Cynthia hastened to set it. I could see she was very much ashamed of having been gone so long. Neither of us knew it was so late. But Miss Hannah said it didn't make a mite o' difference, there was next to nothing to do, and looked at me with a little smile, which said, "You see how it is. I'm the one who has faculty, and I favor her."

I was very hungry; and, though it was not yet six, it seemed a whole day since dinner-time. Miss Hannah made many apologies; and said, if I had only set a day, she would have had things as they ought to be. But it was a very good supper, and she knew it! She didn't know but I was tired o' lobsters. And when I had eaten two of the biscuit, and had begun an attack on the hot gingerbread, she said humbly that she didn't know when she had had such bad luck, though Georgie and I were both satisfied. He did not speak more than once or twice during the meal. I do not think he was afraid of me, for we had had many a lunch together when he had taken me out fishing; but this was an occasion, and there was at first the least possible restraint over all the company, though I'm glad to say it soon vanished. We had two kinds of preserves, and some honey beside, and there was a pie with a pale, smooth crust, and three cuts in the top. It looked like a very good pie of its kind; but one can't eat every thing, though one does one's best. And we had big cups of tea; and, though Miss Hannah supposed I had never eaten with any thing but silver forks before, it happened luckily that I had, and we were very merry indeed. Miss Hannah told us several stories of the time she kept school, and gave us some reminiscences of her life at the Port; and Miss Cynthia looked at me as if she had heard them before, and wished to say, "I know she's having a good time." I think Miss Cynthia felt, after we were out in the woods, as if I were her company, and she was responsible for me.

I thanked them heartily when I came away, for I had had such a pleasant time. Miss Cynthia picked me a huge nosegay of her flowers, and whispered that she hoped I wouldn't forget about lending her the book. Poor woman! she was so young,—only a girl yet, in spite of her having lived more than fifty years in that plain, dull home of hers, in spite of her faded face and her grayish hair. We came away in the rattling wagon. Georgie sat up in his place with a steady hand on the reins, and keeping a careful lookout ahead, as if he were steering a boat through a rough sea.

We passed the house where the auction had been, and it was all shut up. The cat sat on the doorstep waiting patiently, and I felt very sorry for her; but Georgie said there were neighbors not far off, and she was a master hand for squirrels. I was glad to get sight of the sea again, and to smell the first stray whiff of salt air that blew in to meet us as we crossed the marshes. I think the life in me must be next of kin to the life of the sea, for it is drawn toward it strangely, as a little drop of quicksilver grows uneasy just out of reach of a greater one.

"Good-night, Georgie!" said I; and he nodded his head a little as he drove away to take the horse home. "Much obliged to you for my ride," said he, and I knew in a minute that his father or one of the aunts had cautioned him not to forget to make his acknowledgments. He had told me on the way down that he had baited his nets all ready to set that evening. I knew he was in a hurry to go out, and it was not long before I saw his boat pushing off. It was after eight o'clock, and the moon was coming up pale and white out of the sea, while the west was still bright after the clear sunset.

I have a little model of a fishing dory that Georgie made for me, with its sprit-sail and killick and painter and oars and gaff all cleverly cut with the clumsiest of jackknives. I care a great deal for the little boat; and I gave him a better knife before I came away, to remember me by; but I am afraid its shininess and trig shape may have seemed a trifle unmanly to him. His father's had been sharpened on the beach-stones to clean many a fish, and it was notched and dingy; but this would cut; there was no doubt about that. I hope Georgie was sorry when we said good-by. I'm sure I was.

A solemn, careful, contented young life, with none of the playfulness or childishness that belong to it,—this is my little fisherman, whose memory already fades of whatever tenderness his dead mother may have given him. But he is lucky in this, that he has found his work and likes it; and so I say, 'May the sea prove kind to him! and may he find the Friend those other fishermen found, who were mending their nets on the shores of Galilee! and may he make the harbor of heaven by and by after a stormy voyage or a quiet one, whichever pleases God!

A Note About the Author

Sarah Orne Jewett (1849–1909) was a prolific American author and poet from South Berwick, Maine. First published at the age of nineteen, Jewett started her career early, combining her love of nature with her literary talent. Known for vividly depicting coastal Maine settings, Jewett was a major figure in the American literary regionalism genre. Though she never married, Jewett lived and traveled with fellow writer Annie Adams Fields, who supported her in her literary endeavors.

A Note from the Publisher

Spanning many genres, from non-fiction essays to literature classics to children's books and lyric poetry, Mint Edition books showcase the master works of our time in a modern new package. The text is freshly typeset, is clean and easy to read, and features a new note about the author in each volume. Many books also include exclusive new introductory material. Every book boasts a striking new cover, which makes it as appropriate for collecting as it is for gift giving. Mint Edition books are only printed when a reader orders them, so natural resources are not wasted. We're proud that our books are never manufactured in excess and exist only in the exact quantity they need to be read and enjoyed.

bookfinity™

Discover more of your favorite classics with Bookfinity™.

- Track your reading with custom book lists.
- Get great book recommendations for your personalized Reader Type.
- Add reviews for your favorite books.
- AND MUCH MORE!

Visit **bookfinity.com** and take the fun Reader Type quiz to get started.

Enjoy our classic and modern companion pairings!

Printed in the USA
CPSIA information can be obtained
at www.ICGtesting.com
JSHW082358140824
68134JS00020B/2145